THE SHIP THAT SAILED
THE TIME STREAM

*

Joe Rate was captain of the experimental U.S. Navy yawl *Alice*. That day, everything seemed to happen to him. First there had been that freak electrical storm. Then the lightning strike and the time-jump. Thrown a thousand years back in time, they were stranded in the past. With two weeks' provisions. Apart from that, they had boarded a strange ship and ended up with a strange barbarian girl on board. Now the four Viking raiding ships were bearing down on them and the first spears thudding into the foredeck. Definitely a full day.

G. C. Edmondson

The Ship That Sailed
the Time Stream

ARROW BOOKS

ARROW BOOKS LTD
178–202 Great Portland Street, London W 1

AN IMPRINT OF THE HUTCHINSON GROUP

London Melbourne Sydney Auckland
Wellington Johannesburg Cape Town
and agencies throughout the world

*

First published in Great Britain by
Arrow Books 1971

*Made and printed in Great Britain
by The Anchor Press Ltd,
Tiptree, Essex*

ISBN 0 09 004890 3

To Himself, who kept bugging me to write a book.

1

Though he was given to daydreams of a wooden ship and iron men era, Ensign Joseph Rate was captain of a wooden ship in a predominantly atomic navy. And a sailing ship at that!

The *Alice* was an 89-foot yawl, engaged in very secret work which involved countermeasures against enemy submarines. Since the *Alice* could move without thumpings or engine noises, she was well suited for this kind of work. Ensign Joe Rate was less suited to be her skipper.

A year ago he had been one of Dr. Battlement's Bright Young Men, youngest assistant professor in the history of Athosburg College.

At the moment he was arguing with Dr. Krom. 'If we don't start hauling your perverted Christmas tree out right now there won't be time,' he said. 'That squall isn't going to wait.'

Dr. Krom sighed and passed a hand through his shock of white hair. 'We could be through in another hour,' he protested. Joe showed no signs of weakening so the doctor played his trump card. 'Finish these tests today and we'll spend the next two weekends in San Diego.'

A glance at the bulletin board would have advised the old man that Ensign Rate and the *Alice* were already scheduled to spend tomorrow in port. Nothing could have given Joe more pleasure than not doing so.

Joe knew perfectly well Dr. Krom saw him as a navy-minded oaf. He reflected charitably that he didn't regard the doctor as a mad scientist. Feebleminded, perhaps. . . . 'Will you absolve me if we have to cut it loose?' He spoke loud enough to be overheard and repeated come Board of Inquiry day.

'You won't have to,' Dr. Krom said confidently. He was not a meteorologist.

'On thy head be it,' Joe muttered.

Twenty minutes later the yawl was plunging with that corkscrew motion peculiar to sailing hulls when stripped of the canvas which steadies them. Sailors fought to lash the flogging main boom someplace where Dr. Krom's nightmare would not make the yawl list quite so soggily aport and perhaps work a trifle less doggedly at smashing the midships planking.

Krom's Christmas Tree was a fantastic, hydrophone-studded pyramid which was grunted overboard with much winching and taking of the Lord's Name in vain while accomplices in the dinghy exploded half-pound charges of T.N.T. at varying distances. While the Christmas tree draped from the end of the main boom no sail could be set, and the *Alice* listed uncomfortably.

'Be careful,' Dr. Krom begged. 'Two years' appropriation went into that.'

'You'd better go below, sir,' Ensign Rate said.

'But maybe I can help.'

Joe choked back his I-told-you-so as he glanced at the skinny old man. 'Let me handle it,' he said. 'We pay taxes too.' Joe had learned a little about handling superannuated genius back in his History Department days—but not enough.

If getting an education had not exactly meant starving in a garret, still it had not been easy for Joe. Were it not for his phenomenal memory the hours he'd spent keeping body and soul together might have kept the young man from passing a single course. As it was, college had seemed to him a mere variation and expansion on themes he could still quote verbatim from sixth grade texts. But he had never learned how to out-guess Dr. Battlement or his daughter. He wondered if he'd ever be able to handle Dr. Krom.

Ten hectic minutes passed before the *Alice's* boom was secured. Under bare poles and with her diesel barely ticking over, the yawl crabbed into the swell. Krom's monster hung from a hundred feet of cable and would be safe, providing the *Alice* maintained steerageway and didn't drift into shallow water. The squall blew the tops from short, steep waves. A thunderhead drew lightning from a wave-crest a mile away. There hadn't been time for oilskins and Joe was soaked. 'You all right?' he asked. The helmsman nodded so he ducked below.

Gorson and Cookie were fumbling with something inside a bell jar as he passed through the galley. 'Coffee, Skipper?' Cook asked. Joe shook his head. He knew he ought to say something about the still but they had been in the navy longer than he. The chief had a theory that their dried-apple brandy's foul taste came from too much heat—hence their experiments with low temperature vacuum distillation.

He went into his cabin and rummaged for dry clothes. In the galley Cookie humped energetically over a hand vacuum pump while Gorson studied the gleaming copper coil inside the bell jar.

At that moment lightning struck.

Most of the charge bled harmlessly down the *Alice's* standing rigging to the waterline, but there was enough left over to stand everybody's hair on end. Balls of St. Emo's fire danced merrily about the ships innards and the single echoless *CRACK* was felt rather than heard.

In the galley Cookie and Gorson stared at the melted coil which crumpled amid shards of the shattered bell jar. 'Holy balls,' Gorson mumbled, 'Hey Skipper, look!' But

9

Ensign Rate, clad only in non-regulation skivvy drawers, was clambering up the ladder.

Seaman Guilbeau stared glassily at the binnacle. The *Alice* was 90° off course. The ensign pushed him away and fought the struggling yawl back up. Schwartz and Rose, who had been tending the winch, sat up dazedly. Dr. Krom's bushy head emerged from the forward scuttle. 'Stop worrying,' Joe called. 'Your monster's still with us.' He glanced upward to see how much of the *Alice's* standing rigging had been cremated by the flash. There were no loose stays dangling. No one was dead. He reached for a cigarette and abrupty learned he was only drawers distant from naked.

The squall was dying now and Joe was troubled by a feeling that something was wrong. Then he knew what it was: the wind was blowing from the wrong direction.

Freedy came on deck. 'Radio's dead,' he reported.

'Both ways?'

The radioman shrugged. 'Nothing coming in. Can't tell if I'm getting out.'

The bos'n came on deck and took the wheel. Joe herded the dazed deck watch below. Cookie was sweeping up the shattered bell jar when he passed through the galley. 'Any other damage?' the cook asked. Joe shook his head and went into his cabin to finish dressing.

'Mr. Rate—hey, Joe!' Gorson screamed. The skipper abandoned his coffee and scrambled on deck again. The bos'n was staring at a ship off the port bow. It was also a wooden ship, with a single furled square sail. Bearded faces stared from behind shields which lined the side. An armoured and helmeted man braced himself at the dragon figurehead and chanted as oars flashed.

'A fine day to be shooting a movie,' Joe growled.

The actors shipped oars and drifted toward the *Alice*. 'How'd you make out in the squall?' Joe shouted.

The man in the bow yelled back. Joe didn't understand

him. He yelled again. When Joe didn't understand a second time the bright bearded man threw a spear. It landed with a thunk and stood thrilling in the after scuttle. 'Hey, take it easy,' Joe yelled, 'That's navy property! What studio do you guys work for anyway?'

Abruptly, bearded and armoured oarsmen stood behind the bulwark and more spears winged toward the *Alice*. Gorson's mouth opened and he flattened himself in the foot-deep cockpit.

'I knew all actors were nuts,' Joe muttered. 'But this's carrying Stanislavsky too damn far!'

Helmeted men crowded into the Viking's ship's bow, blandishing halfmoon axes. The ships were only fifty feet apart now. Joe scrambled from behind the binnacle and rammed the throttle forward. The diesel roared and the *Alice* strained for her full ten knots. But something was wrong. She wasn't answering her helm properly.

Gorson sat up. 'Oh no!' he moaned. Krom's Christmas tree still dangled a hundred feet below the *Alice's* port side. Straining against it, the *Alice* swung hard aport—straight for the boatload of spearhappy actors. Gorson and Joe knocked each other down in their scramble for the reversing lever. There was a splintering noise as the *Alice* knifed into lapstrake planking. The two men looked at each other. 'Shall we jump overboard arm in arm?' Joe asked.

But things were not finished. Robbed of forward momentum, the *Alice* belatedly answered her reversing gear. As she backed away water rushed into the hole in the other ship. Men were boiling out of the *Alice's* hatches now and the *Alice*, still shackled to Krom's Christmas tree, was doing her level best to swing full circle and ram her stern into the Viking ship's opposite side. And the reversing gear was stuck again!

Joe had to throttle down before he could kick it into forward. Water boiled under her stern and the yawl stopped a scant dozen feet from a second collision. Gorson meanwhile had sprinted to the winch and was lowering Krom's Christmas tree to give the *Alice* a longer tether.

The Viking ship was settling on an even keel and Joe realised he would have to cut Krom's nightmare loose if he hoped to save any of the actors. He hoped the wetting would cure some of their rambunctiousness. And what had gotten into the Coast Guard to let a hundred armour-clad men go asea in this overgrown canoe without so much as a life jacket between them?

He grabbed a life ring and flung it Vikingward. The bearded actor shied away as if it were radioactive. Finally one picked it up gingerly with his sword point and dropped it over the side.

A double bladed axe whizzed and clattered to a stop beside Gorson. The chief had had enough. He picked it up and swung. Sheaves squealed and the yawl righted herself as two years of Dr. Krom's appropriation and a hundred feet of the *Alice's* cable gurgled downward. The yawl abruptly took a reasonable attitude toward steering.

Dr. Krom opened and closed his mouth like a freshly boated cod but the bos'n still weighed the axe in one hairy paw.

The armour-ballasted actors made surprisingly little outcry. The longship gave a final gurgle and left floating oars by way of epitaph. In an hour Joe supposed he'd be sick but at the moment it was simply unbelievable. Half the actors had gone down with their crackerbox ship. He headed back to pick up those who still clung to oars and water kegs. They yelled things which sounded vaguely Scandinavian and definitely insulting. As the *Alice* approached each man let go of whatever he held and let his armour pull him down. Stanislavsky to the last, Joe decided. He wondered what he was going to say before the inevitable Board of Inquiry.

'See if Freedy's done anything with the radio,' he said. Gorson nodded and went below. Joe pulled the cam lifter and the diesel sneezed itself to death. 'Drop anchor,' he called. There was a rattle of chain.

'No bottom, sir,' Seaman Guilbeau reported moments later.

'You're kidding.'

'No ah ain', sir.' The little Cajun was emphatic.

Ensign Rate took a wild look around the horizon. The coast was hidden in a haze. He dived down the cabin scuttle.

'Still dead,' Freedy reported. 'Can't find anything wrong but all I get is static.'

'Try the fathometer.'

The radioman flipped switches until a needle inked across a sheet of graph paper. All the way across! He switched to the next range. Again the recorder pinned itself. He switched again and shrugged. 'Damned lightning must've ruined everything. There's no place that deep within fifty miles of San Diego.'

Since the *Alice* was required to anchor under unusual circumstances her chain was extended with a hundred fathoms of hot-stretch nylon. 'We're all out and no bottom,' Joe said. Freedy looked at him unhappily. They went on deck where Dr. Krom was pacing like the caricature of an expectant father.

'Drifting,' the little man wailed. 'We'll never find it again.'

Joe told him about the fathometer.

'Impossible,' Krom said. 'I corrected the charts for most of this area myself.'

'All right, so you're an expert. What does an anchor cable all out and dangling straight down mean?' Joe studied his watch and then the sky. The squall had blown itself out but the breeze still came at them wrong. 'Look at the binnacle,' he said.

The old man studied the compass and frowned.

'What time have you?' Joe persisted.

'2 p.m.'

'Pacific Standard?'

'Naturally.'

'Look,' Joe said. The sun was barely visible through thin clouds. The doctor frowned as he looked from sun to compass. 'Are you suggesting we've lost three hours?'

'Either in time or in longitude. And now, if you'll excuse me, I'm going to get the book out and learn how to take a noon shot.'

An hour later the *Alice* still drifted with one man on deck. Seven sailors, Dr. Krom, and his civilian assistant, sat around the galley table. Ensign Rate cleared his throat. 'My noon shot places us way north of where we ought to be. I'll get a star sight tonight and pinpoint the latitude. As for longitude, we could be anywhere.'

Seaman Guilbeau squirmed. 'Ain't we gonna be in San Diego tonight, sir?'

Rate shook his head. For the last couple of hours a wild suspicion had been growing on him. 'How're we fixed for food?' he asked.

Cook's Adam's apple bobbed twice. 'We're supposed to be in Dago tomorrow,' he protested.

'Well, we won't be. Now how much've we got?'

Cook shrugged his thin shoulders. 'I dunno; maybe ten days.'

'Were the water tanks topped up before we left?'

Gorson nodded. 'Enough for two weeks, providing the shower's secured.'

'It is as of this moment. How about fuel?'

MM3/c Abe Rose mouthed his cigar. 'Enough for forty hours cruising.'

Joe pushed his cap back to an improper angle. 'Providing Cook goes easy on the stove, I suppose?'

The engineman nodded. 'Everything runs off the same tank.'

'All right. Now, I don't want to harp on this, but it's hard telling when we'll see any more food, water or oil. From now on if you need a bath use a bucket of brine on deck. It takes fuel to charge batteries so douse the record player. No lights unless they're absolutely necessary. Cookie, what's in the refrigerator?'

'The usual stuff—milk, eggs, meat and butter.'

'How about dry provisions and canned goods?'

'You know the navy,' the cook said. 'Flour, beans, Spam and fruit.'

'All right. Use up the perishables first. As soon's the box's empty, secure it. That'll save a little fuel.'

Cook nodded. 'But what happened? How'd we get so far from San Diego?'

Seaman Schwartz stuck his unlovely face down the scuttle. 'Something in sight,' he said. Everyone followed Rate up the ladder.

The ship was about a mile away, sailing on a beam reach. 'Came heading straight toward us out of the fog,' Schwartz said. 'Soon's they caught sight of us they sheered off. But what is it?'

Ensign Rate studied the lines of the retreating ship. He'd never actually seen one before but he thought he knew what it was. He cringed at the idea of wasting electricity on the heels of his economy lecture but he could think of no way to bring in a hundred fathoms of anchor line without using the electric winch.

While it was whirring in they hoisted the jigger. It was the first time Rate had ever set sail without using the engine to keep a heading into the wind. He hoped the flat sheeted jigger would be enough to weathercock the yawl while the mains'l was being winched up. It was, and by the time the last fathom of chain rattled through the winch the Alice was under all plain sail and chasing the stranger.

After a moment's internal debate Joe decided against setting the spinnaker. They could probably catch the

15

stubby little merchantman without it and he didn't want to worry about hundreds of yards of flapping canvas, should they have come about suddenly.

Visibility was still less than two miles and the ship had disappeared several minutes ago. Joe thought about firing up the radar but he didn't want to waste power. He'd sail an hour toward where they had disappeared first. He took the helm himself and tried to piece together what he knew about the other ship and the men who sailed her.

Dr. Krom lit his pipe. 'Looked like something out of the Hanseatic League,' he guessed. All hands crowded aft into the cockpit, eager for any scrap of information.

'It's not a Hanse ship,' Joe said.

Dr. Krom raised his eyebrows. He hadn't really expected this navy-minded oaf to know what he was talking about.

Joe took a deep breath. 'The ship we're following,' he began, 'is a knarr. They averaged eighty to ninety feet, carried a single square sail on a short, heavily shrouded mast. Bow and stern are pierced for eight oars which are used only when docking. The decking amidships is removable to load cargo.'

Every time Joe made one of these impromptu lectures he was dogged by the suspicion that he was a showoff—the kind of pompous fraud who'd shill for a rigged quiz show. He knew perfectly well he wasn't a genius; he was merely cursed with a good memory. But even Dr. Krom was impressed so he continued. 'My noon shot placed us on a latitude corresponding to the Gulf of Finland, Davis Straits, Hudson Bay, the Bering Sea or the North Atlantic. The knarr was used to transport merchandise from and to Iceland and the longship, according to all the books, was used only on raids between the Scandinavian peninsula and the British Isles. Since knarrs bound for Iceland commonly took their departure from the Shetlands or the Orkneys, I'd guess we're somewhere north of Scotland. And in time, we must be somewhere between nine and twelve hundred A.D.'

'Whooee, Mr. Rate, what's a smaht man like you doin' in the navy?'

Joe eyed the little Cajun sadly. What indeed? As a boy he had patiently cluttered his mind with useless facts for it was axiomatic that education brought wealth and position. Once in a while he'd wondered a trifle worriedly how all this was to come about. Meanwhile, he'd read more history than was required. It was the only reading he did strictly for kicks. He'd felt guilty about this for his father had often told Joe that one never acquired wealth and position by having fun.

And then Dr. Battlement had channelled the young man's aimless reading by painting glowing pictures of the academic life. Joe decided to become a professor.

Various factors entered into this watering down of the young man's dream. There was his aptitude for languages, his love of history, and his absolute incapacity to find any joy in transferring dollars from one ledger to another via the legal loopholery of modern business.

The decision was not, of course, arrived at overnight. There were mornings of chill self-analysis while shivering through Naval ROTC drill. It was an inch by inch retreat from cherished, if undefined, dreams—a battle which ended in capitulation when increasingly frantic study of want ads during his final semester showed no openings for historians or specialists in dead languages.

Joe became an assistant. His future was assured. In ten years his salary would climb nearly to that of a union plumber. But there were other things entailed in being one of Dr. Battlement's Bright Young Men. Even professors cast desirous looks on the opposing sex. Worse still, they have been known to marry and procreate their kind. Dr. Battlement had a daughter.

Ariadne Battlement was small, dark, and protective. Her capable hands were forever refolding her handkerchief in a father's pocket or straightening the tie of a Bright Young Man. Joe rather liked her.

But when invitations to dine with the Battlements became frequent he turned restive. When Ariadne started sewing his buttons and turning his collars the young man panicked. After a night of floor pacing and soul searching he controlled his first blind impulse to hop a freight. When the office opened at 8 o'clock Joe was there.

'I want to join the navy,' he had said.

The *Alice* was making eight and a half knots under all plain sail. Her crew were making countless decibels, playing endless variations on 'Impossible; couldn't happen to us!' 'What more proof do you need?' Joe asked. 'Those lads we rammed were playing for keeps. And Freedy can't fix the radio. Can you?'

Freedy shook his head.

'There's nothing wrong with it; just no station to hear or answer us.' Joe sighed. They were shocked but he still couldn't make them believe it. Dr. Krom mumbled something.

'We'll have our final proof soon.' Joe studied his watch. They had been sailing across the wind for fifty minutes. 'Was the yard squared when they first saw us?' he asked. Schwartz nodded. 'They were running straight before the wind.'

Joe knew he was building a case on very little evidence but the knarr was probably bound for Iceland. The Norse had only seen the *Alice* with sails furled and could have no idea of her true speed. They had merely operated on the fine old premise that a stranger was an enemy and taken evasive tactics. Once out of sight they would probably revert to their original course. He wondered if the Norse sailors had an hourglass aboard.

Fifty-eight minutes ticked up on his watch. 'Slack sheets,' Joe yelled. With the main boom straight out the blanketed jib hung limp and the yawl tended to yaw like a drunken skater from the unbalanced push of main and jigger.

'There they are!' Villegas yelled. 'Dead ahead.'

Joe felt the wave of admiration which passed through his crew. He was acutely aware of his status as a boot ensign and tried to show no emotion. 'All hands lay aft,' he called.

'Something tells me,' he began, 'that we're going to need an interpreter. How many languages have we among us?'

There was silence.

'Gorson?'

'Sir?' It was the first 'sir' Ensign Rate had ever extracted from the bos'n.

'How about you? Norwegian or Swede?'

The bos'n spread his hands. 'Used to understand it. I dunno any more.'

'Guilbeau, you speak something that might pass for French. The Cajun nodded. 'Cook?'

'Cain't even talk English good,' the cook shrugged.

'Rose?'

'If they're Hebrews I'm your man,' the engineman offered.

'Schwartz?'

'Don't look at me,' Seaman Schwartz said.

'McGrath?' McGrath shook his head.

'Freedy?'

'No, sir,' the radioman said.

Joe sighed. More and more it stemed he was going to have to carry the ball. He turned to the civilians. 'How about you, Dr. Krom?'

'Russian, French, German and Hungarian,' the oceanographer said.

'No Latin or Greek?'

'They were not required for my speciality.'

'Lapham?'

Dr. Krom's assistant was a hornrimmed type straight

from college who had infiltrated the lab's personnel via its summer employment programme. Twenty-five percent of his time aboard the *Alice* was spent struggling with his queasy stomach. The other seventy-five percent, he was actively seasick. 'Pig Latin?' the unhappy young man offered.

A stern chase is always a long chase but to Joe it was not long enough. An hour halved the distance between them and the knarr and he still had not the slightest idea what he would do when the eventual meeting took place.

Mixed in with much other reading of ancient source materials, Joe had once struggled through the old Icelandic cycle and the Jomsviking Saga in parallel columns of Old Norse and Modern English. Though admirable for literary and teaching purposes, Joe suspected that his Old Norse would prove sadly lacking when it came to more mundane matters. He tried desperately to recall a few words. Would the men aboard the knarr parley or would they come out swinging like the longship Vikings? He hoped not. The bad actors must have been raiding England or Ireland and spoiling for a fight anyway.

He caught Gorson's eye and they went below together. 'Aside from the rifle and my pistol, what've we got in the way of weapons?'

The bos'n thought a moment. 'You mean like spears? Say, if we're really back a thousand years they won't have guns, will they?'

Joe shook his head. 'No gunpowder. There was Greek fire but I doubt if these people will have it. We'll face axes, swords, maybe bows and arrows.'

'What're we going to do when we catch them?'

Joe experimented with an omniscient smile; then he collapsed. 'Nothing in the book covers this situation,' he said flatly, 'But I'd like to know for sure where we are. Say, are there any charts for the North Atlantic?'

'Pilot charts for all five oceans,' Gorson said, 'But nothing that'd be any help getting in and out of a harbour.'

'Oh great!' Joe moaned.

'We're getting close, sir,' Villegas called down the scuttle.

It was late afternoon by now and from the way the low wheeling sun swung north Joe guessed they must be near midsummer. 'Bring the flare pistol,' he told Gorson. The stubby knarr was shorter than the *Alice* but her broad beam and blunt fore and aft sections gave her a much greater carrying capacity. 'We'll come up on her starboard side,' Joe said. 'Better hang out some fenders.'

They came within a hundred yards of the knarr and Joe faced a new problem: the *Alice* was moving twice as fast. If they grappled something would be torn out by the roots. The *Alice* ripped along, passing within twenty feet of the other ship. They caught rapid glimpses of a balding, red-faced man at the helm. Bright bearded men and a pair of boys stared at them. Joe was surprised to see several women aboard. A dark-haired girl knelt before the fire which blazed in a sandbox amidships.

Seaman Villegas gave a wolf howl. '*Ay mamacita, que linda eres!*' he panted. The girl looked up sharply. She was still looking when they passed hailing distance.

A mile ahead the *Alice* turned into the wind and dropped her mains'l. Hove to under jib and jigger they waited for the knarr to catch up. Rate half expected the vessel to sheer off and try to lose them again but the dumpy merchantman wallowed steadily forward. Then he understood why: there were at least thirty men aboard the knarr and its master had seen only eleven aboard the *Alice*. He was ready to trade or fight. Joe wished he knew which.

He gave the rifle to Cook. The gaunt Tennessean was the only crew member who had ever been known to hit anything with it. Irrelevantly, Joe wondered if his cook had ever target practised on revenooers. He kept the pistol for himself.

The summer sun was still high but clouds were obscuring it again. The *Alice* carried a floodlight in her shrouds for handling the winch after dark. Joe thought of turning it on for whatever 'magical' effect it might have on medieval minds. He decided not to—it might scare them away. Worse, under its glare they would be perfect targets if the Northmen did not scare.

The knarr brailed up its sail and drifted gently toward them. It bumped and ground for a moment at the fenders suspended over the *Alice's* side. Sailors on both ships tossed lines and fended off with oars and boat hooks. Joe took a deep breath. 'Here goes,' he said, and jumped aboard.

The skipper of the knarr stood stiffly at the steering oar. He showed no signs of moving, so Joe walked aft. He wondered about the protocol of the situation. It might have been better to stand on his dignity and make the other man board the *Alice*. The red-bearded man wore skintight *leistrabraekr* which exaggerated his incipient pot. The loose, ill-fitting blouse gave him a top-heavy look.

He scowled ferociously over flowing moustaches whose tips were several shades whiter from lime bleaching. As Joe approached he held his awkward leaning posture on the steering oar. 'Hvar är vi?' Joe asked, hoping he was pronouncing the words right. Whiskers stared at him. He tried another tack. 'Danamark?' Another stare.

'Erin?'

'Angleland?'

'Scotland?' Silence.

'Shetland? Orkney? Iceland?' Joe asked desperately.

Whiskers was losing patience. He roared something and as the sword flashed Joe suddenly understood why the man had leaned and kept his hand behind him on the steering oar. Though he had half expected some such thing, the swiftness of Whiskers' assault surprised Joe. He saw with instant clarity that the Northman would bisect him before he could begin to draw the pistol.

Then a look of blank surprise filled the skipper's broad face. He slumped back over the oar. The sword slipped from his hand and clattered to the deck. *Good old Cookie*, Joe thought. But he hadn't heard the rifle go off. He glanced back at the *Alice* and felt sudden shame at his imbecility. No wonder Cook hadn't fired. He was standing directly in front of the Northman.

The red-bearded man arched backward over the oar and made distressing noises. As the sloppy blouse pulled tight Joe saw the knife handle protruding from Whiskers' solar plexus.

A girl burst through the crowd of starers amidships and lunged at Joe. He nearly beaned her with the revolver before he realised she was not attacking. '*Amparo!*' the girl screamed. 'Rescue me from these pagans!'

Her language was archaic but time does little damage to Mediterranean tongues. The modern day Spaniard reads the exploits of El Cid without difficulty whereas 10th Century English sounds more like German.

'For two years I am slave to these pagans. When you hailed in my language I knew the time for vengeance had come. I made ready the knife.'

People amidships were beginning to recover. Joe saw the weapons they had been hiding. In a moment they would rush him. The girl lay at his feet, her arms around his knees. Joe guessed he was already half a god. He raised his arms like an Old Testament prophet and began a sonorous chant:

'Gorson, thou whoreson,
Get the flare gun ready
At the count of five,
Fire it straight up.
One.'

He bowed deeply and straightened, thrusting his arms heavenward again. 'Two.' He bowed again. 'Three, four.' From the corner of his eye he saw frantic activity on the deck of the *Alice*. *Neptune help us if we can't find it,* Joe thought— and said, 'Five!'

There was a pop and hissing roar. Under the dazzle of a parachute flare Joe saw the last of the fight go out of the Northmen.

'What cargo?' he asked the girl.

'In truth, my lord, I do not know,' he said. 'It was loaded before my mistress took me aboard.'

'Do you speak their language? Oh for heaven's sake, stand up!' He undid her clutch from his knees and pulled the girl upright. She was small and dark but there her resemblance to the capable Ariadne Battlement ended. The shapeless grey woollen dress would have been prim and decorous on a girl several years younger and smaller but now it bulged in all the proper places. In fact, it threatened to burst in a couple of them. Her long loose hair was of the blackest black but her face was not spoiled with the coarseness so often found among Spanish Gypsy women. It was a demure little face with surprisingly large eyes which gazed up at Joe with the humble adoration of a cocker spaniel. Joe felt protective instincts starting to tingle all through him.

He remembered with something of a shock that this fragile creature had just skewered the steersman and only incidentally saved his life. 'I understand something of the pagan tongue,' she said.

'Who's the—' He couldn't think of the word for first mate. '*El número dos,*' he finished lamely.

She pointed at a sandy-haired giant with a beard and moustache nearly as ferocious as the dead captain's. Joe beckoned with a peremptory thumb. The giant stared at him. 'Tell him,' Joe instructed, 'to come here or I'll call down lightning.'

24

She spoke in fluting gurgles until the giant came running. 'Where to, where from, and what cargo?' Joe asked. She interpreted again and the giant mumbled an answer. They were out of Orkney, bound for Iceland, and with a mixed cargo.

'How far out?'

'Two days.'

'What're the women and children doing aboard?'

The girl spat. 'They couldn't stick Olaf's new law.'

Joe's ears pricked up. 'Olaf Tryggvasson?'

The girl nodded.

The Norwegian king had forced even the distant Icelanders to turn Christian in the year 1000. This must be 990 something or other. 'You know the date?' he asked.

'I was taken in the 12th year of Almanzor.'

History was full of Arab kings named Mansour; Joe wondered which one she meant. 'How many years since the birth of Christ?' he asked.

'How should I know?' the girl shrugged.

The first mate still waited. 'Tell him to start getting some provisions on deck.'

The Northman's answer was brief.

'He says trading ships are immune to plunder by Viking law. Since you choose to disregard the rules of civilised warfare you can kill him now and load your own *gurgle* loot.'

Joe decided not to ask what the untranslated gurgle meant. 'If he'd respected my life,' he said, 'I would have respected his cargo. As it is, I'll leave him provisions to reach port. If he holds his mouth right I may leave him enough teeth to eat them.'

A look of disappointment crossed the girl's face.

'But,' Joe added hastily, 'any funny business and I'll turn you and that knife loose.' He hoped the girl would interpret properly. Chances were she'd garble it just for the hell of it. But apparently she didn't. The tall man turned and bellowed orders.

In a moment the midships planking was up and men passed coarse woollen sacks of rye over the *Alice's* rail. Joe would, he imagined, soon be sick of rye bread but they could live a long time on it, providing he located fresh vegetables. 'Do you bake aboard ship?' he asked the girl. She waggled her finger in a Latin 'no' and Joe suddenly remembered how the Norse used to bake hardtack all winter —chewy as a phonograph record and just about as tasty.

The *Alice* didn't have so much as a coffee grinder aboard. How, Joe wondered, would they make flour? As a small mountain of rye piled up on the yawl's deck he calculated that they couldn't possibly use more than fifteen pounds a day. That meant a hundred and thirty-three days to the ton. There must already be four tons aboard the yawl. 'Enough,' he shouted. He pointed a finger at the first mate. 'Stay there or I'll turn you into a pumpkin,' he threatened, and began exploring the knarr.

There were twenty scrawny, athletic sheep in a pen up forward. Joe took eight. Below he found bolts of heavy woollen cloth. It would bag and shrink horribly but the knarr's sails seemed to be made of it. Joe shuddered to think what some really heavy weather would do to the *Alice's* ancient canvas. He took half the cloth. He checked the knarr's water butts and decided no. Green streamers were visible through the bungholes and they were only two days out!

He found his real treasure in the knarr's dinghy: a small pair of millstones tied together made up the small boat's anchor. He was ready to leave when another necessity caught his eye. He took half the firewood too.

'You know,' he said apologetically as they left the knarr, 'we probably won't be heading for Spain.' He'd been about to ask the girl if she wouldn't rather stay with the Norse when he realised what would happen to her the moment he left. 'But you're welcome aboard,' he added.

'You're Christian?'

'Most of us, I guess.'

'I have a few things.' The girl gave instructions in Norse. The first mate shouted all hands in line and the girl went down the line, pausing before each woman like a boot ensign on his first inspection. While the *Alice's* men watched awedly, women began undressing. The man gathered their clothes and passed the bundle on board the *Alice*. The girl paused again before the naked, shivering women. Pausing before one, she drew the knife. Slowly, and with great deliberation, she incised a bloody cross into the older woman's forehead. The woman glared unblinking while another cross was etched in each cheek.

Joe stared fascinated, wanting to stop this ritual but unable to make himself move. After all, the girl had saved his life. It's a barbarous era, he reflected—and what must that old woman have been doing to the girl for the last two years?

Tenderly, and with loving care, the dark haired girl inscribed another X on her former owner's belly. The older woman stood erect, her hawk face expressionless. The girl stood back to admire her work and with a lightning movement, planted a kick in the middle of the X. The Norse woman doubled up in silence.

2

They left the naked Norse women feeling some joy at finding themselves still unraped. Joe tacked for an hour so the knarr, which couldn't sail upwind for sour apples, would not be tempted to try any devilry under cover of darkness. There was still light to read by. They slacked sheets and the yawl settled down on a SW course.

And now, what was he going to do with the girl? In storybook situations the fair damsel was always installed in the captain's quarters and the skipper played musical chairs with his officers. But the *Alice* was already crowded; she had bunks for the captain and eight men. The two civilians slept in the galley table settees. Plotting board charts, and other indispensables, all were located in Joe's small cubicle. After some thought he curtained off a corner of the forecastle and hoped ten men watching each other would prevent nature from taking its course.

As if he didn't have enough on his mind, now Cookie was plucking his sleeve. 'Cain't burn wood,' he was saying, 'That stove's made for diesel oil.'

The engineman stuck his head up through the cabin sole and wriggled out of the engine compartment.

'Can you make this stove burn wood?' Joe asked.

Rose mouthed his cigar stub thoughtfully. 'I'll try.'

'If you can't, put a tub on deck with a few fathoms of chain in it. Whatever you do, keep it alee and don't set the sails afire.'

The engineman removed a stove lid and surveyed the oil burner's sooty innards.

The girl was dogging Joe, bumping into him each time he turned around. Her name was Raquel. He wondered if she was typical Tenth Century of if her gamy odour came from cramped shipboard conditions. 'Villegas!' he called.

Seaman Villegas rolled out of his bunk and staggered blearily aft.

'Can you understand this savage?'

Villegas eyed her. 'If the dame's from Spain we'll make out,' he said.

'Rig a shelter on deck. Get her a bucket and some soap. She's probably never seen it before, so—'

'Always happy to oblige,' Villegas said.

'You don't have to scrub her back,' Joe said firmly. 'Just explain what soap is.' He retreated into his cabin before anybody else could buttonhole him.

The only chart which promised to be of any use was No. 1400W. The Hydrographic Office's pilot chart of the North Atlantic was printed on oiled silk and someone had been using it for a tablecloth. He scrubbed at the coffee stain which circumnavigated Ireland and tried to guess where they were.

If the knarr was two days northwest of the Orkneys there should be little danger. He fired up the fathometer for a moment to be sure they were beyond the hundred-fathom curve and decided to stay on a southwest course. He went on deck to see if it was dark enough for a star sight. Someone was giggling in the darkness up near the bow.

'Just remember penicillin's a thousand years away,' Joe said grimly. A sheep baa'd in the sudden silence.

He got his sight and made the correction, trying to remember if Polaris had been nearer or farther from true north a thousand years ago. A degree or so farther, he guessed. In any event, the *Alice* was on a latitude somewhere between the Orkneys and Northern Scotland. Until he made a landfall and an arbitrary chronometer setting there would be no way to calculate longitude. He'd have to steer well west where there was less chance of piling into something after dark. Also, he decided, the farther west they ran, the less chance of running into more Vikings.

He left McGrath and Schwartz on deck. Howard Mc-Grath, in addition to being a good steersman, was a Bible student. For reasons known only to God he was also a firm friend of Red Schwartz, whose main interests were fighting and boozing. Though they never made a liberty together, McGrath was always ready to put down his Bible and listen disapprovingly to Schwartz's tales of high adventure.

Gorson and Dr. Krom were drinking coffee when Joe went below. 'Well?' Dr. Krom asked.

'Well what?' Joe wished the old man would go soak his head.

'What're we going to do?'

'I don't know about you,' Joe grunted, 'But I'm going to bed. May the Bureau of Ships have mercy on the man who wakes me before we sight something!'

He woke with a start as the *Alice's* motion changed. The short northern night was over and a bright sun hung high. He scrambled into his pants and rushed on deck. Spray wet him as they ploughed into a swell. An unhappy sheep was complaining in the bow. The wind had changed and the deck watch was sheeting in to make good. 'Let her out a little,' Rate said 'Hold her south-south-west.'

Seaman Guilbeau looked worriedly at him. 'Ain't we headin' for the States, sir?' he asked.

'No,' Joe growled, resisting a temptation to mimic the Cajun's accent. 'We'll let the Indians fight it out among themselves.' He glanced at the sun. It would be at least six hours before he could get a noon shot. Even then it would be worthless, since he still didn't know the date. There was probably some way to calculate a relation between noon shots and the star sight he'd taken last night but after a moment's reflection Joe decided the mathematics was beyond him.

Gorson and Dr. Krom sat staring morosely into coffee mugs when he descended into the galley. They didn't look like they'd changed position since last night. 'All right,' he said to the CPO, 'you may as well get everybody in here who's not on watch.'

Gorson nodded and yelled his way through the forecastle. A minute later Ensign Rate faced the assembled ship's company. 'We have two problems,' he began. 'To stay alive, and to get back to our time. There's no point in trying to go home. In the first place, there's no Panama Canal so we'd have to make a passage around the Horn. Once back in San Diego we could spend our lives easting acorns and fraternising with Digger Indians. Anyone want to?'

There were no volunteers.

'Now, we have a couple of scientists among us,' Joe continued.

'I'm an oceanographer,' Dr. Krom protested. 'I know nothing of time travel.'

'Who does? We're going to need peace and quiet—a place to experiment without having to fight off irate natives. The Tenth Century wasn't noted for its hospitality, though. No matter where we go, we'll wind up in some local feud or get ouselves burnt for witchcraft.'

The ship's company looked unhappily at him.

'What do you suggest?' Dr. Krom asked.

'We need a harbour—preferably some island without local politics to worry us. Once we settle down, maybe we can figure things out.' Raquel sat at one end of the table, eyeing the proceedings with interest. She had changed to a cleaner and better fitting dress, which, to masculine eyes, was not nearly so interesting.

'Were you considering Madeira?' Dr. Krom asked.

'I can't remember whether or not it's inhabitated. The Canaries are out. They had an aboriginal population—I think they were called Gaunches. But the Portuguese explorers found the Azores uninhabited 400 years from now. There's anchorage, water, vegetation, and if worse comes to worse, we can raise mutton.' He looked about the table for signs of disagreement.

Lapham was somewhat greener than usual. 'Isn't there any land closer?' he asked plaintively.

'You need to get your mind off your stomach,' Joe suggested. 'How about pooling your electronic talents with Rose? Maybe the two of you can come up with a wind charger.'

The conference broke up and sailors off watch went back to the sack. In spite of the bright sunshine the weather was raw, with a dampness that penetrated even the newest pea jacket. At least they were driving south, Rate consoled himself. He wondered how soon they'd hit warmer weather. He wished desperately for a gyro compass, but the yawl had none. With radio direction finders navigation had been reduced to the simplest kind of plotting. Only now there were no beacons to plot from. He would have to check the compass deviation against the star for even the BuShips knew not how the magnetic pole had wandered since 1000.

The day wore on and the *Alice* drove steadily south, Raquel came on deck in still another dress, this time with a tight bodice and a skirt which flared to conceal her bare feet. Her hair was tortured into a saladlike crown of pins and brooches. 'What's that?' she inquired, pointing at Joe's binoculars.

'They help me see farther.'

She grabbed them and put them to her eyes. The strap was still around Joe's neck so she had to come very close. Her hair had a warm, clean smell which excited him as no perfumery ever could. Murderous savage, he told himself, but he let her lead him about by the strap as Raquel played with her new toy. If she remembered he was on the other end of the strap she gave no sign.

He was smelling her hair again when she shrieked and dropped the glasses. The strap gave Joe's neck a gallows-thump and he guessed he should have warned her not to look at the sun. He helped her toward the scuttle, wondering how it would feel to carry her down a ladder but half-way there her eyes stopped smarting and she made the ladder under her own power. When he reached the galley she was gone.

Dr. Krom came down and drew a mug of coffee. He passed a hand through bushy white hair and stared morosely at Joe. After a moment he looked around and saw they were alone. 'Was there something you wished to discuss in confidence?' he asked.

Joe shrugged. 'I have no secrets.'

'But you take it so calmly,' the old man said. 'Is this something which happens every day? You know, with these idiotic security regulations one can't know what's going on in other fields.'

Calm! Joe thought. *As if every historian had a shot at getting this close to the Tenth Century!* He couldn't think of what to say to as . . . perceptive . . . a question as Krom's, so he didn't bother to reply. A short silence fell between them.

Finally, Krom asked, 'How soon should we reach the Azores?'

'If the wind holds we might be there in three weeks.'

The old man was silent for a moment. 'I can't get over it,' he said, 'that such a thing should happen to us!'

'What makes you think we're the only ones?'

Dr. Krom looked up sharply.

'You're an oceanographer, Doctor—surely you know how many ships disappear each year.'

'Never to see America again,' the old man muttered. He caught up Joe's argument. 'I disagree most emphatically,' he said in his lecture room voice. 'They've never showed up again in the wrong time.'

'Are you sure?' What alterations have we made on history? One load of Vikings gone without trace, one merchant ship set upon by pirates. What are we? A lot of outlandish foreigners who practise witchcraft. History's filled with birds of that feather. Besides,' Joe continued, 'have we any reason to believe everyone is displaced into the past?'

Jack Lapham came down the ladder, a shade less green than usual. 'How's the wind charger going?' Joe asked.

'I started a sketch and before I was half done your engineman had figured out three improvements.'

'There is nothing like working with one's hands to instill a sense of practicality,' Dr. Krom observed. He was back worrying at Joe's theorising. 'If they came from the past into the future wouldn't we have anachronisms in our time?'

'Possibly,' Joe conceded.

'Then why haven't they been found?' the old man triumphed.

'Perhaps they're doing the same thing we are.'

The old man grew thoughtful. Any sailor who found himself in a strange place, surrounded by ships and people he didn't understand, would have done the same: laid low and hoped for the best.

'But you're implying that the process is reversible,' Lapham said.

'Conservation of energy and all that jazz,' Joe said. 'Doesn't your modern physics make all processes reversible?'

'Then we can get back!'

'I think so.'

'Ah, the confidence of youth,' Dr. Krom said heavily.

'Weren't you ever young?' Joe asked.

34

'A very long time ago,' the oceanographer said, and Joe noticed his accent had grown perceptibly thicker. He regarded the old man speculatively for a moment.

'I read somewhere that you grew up in a very small village,' Joe said.

Krom nodded.

'Well, my engineman's busy rigging a charger so we can use the lights and refrigerator. I was wondering if you and Jack could figure a way to get those millstones turning. Sooner or later we'll need flour.'

'Rye bread!' Krom exclaimed, and in a welling up of half-remembered smells he was suddenly young.

Joe went on deck, leaving the two civilians sketching excitedly on bits of paper towel. The sun still shone and the wind seemed to be holding steady. In spite of the chill Guilbeau was stripped to the waist as he struggled with the yawl's wheel. 'All hands set the spinnaker,' Joe shouted.

As soon as it was dark he took a sight and worked out their latitude. Then he went back on deck and shot the North Star again. Then he went below and told Freedy to fire up the fathometer.

'Sixty fathoms,' Freedy reported a moment later.

'God!' Rate muttered.

'Something wrong, sir?'

'Not exactly,' Joe explained. 'Just better time than I'd expected. We're nearly down to Ireland already, so we'd better head west until we drop off the hundred fathom curve. That's the penalty for not knowing the date: no way to figure longitude except by feeling your way along the bottom.'

He went back on deck and settled the *Alice* on her new course. 'Take a sounding every ten minutes and wake me,' he said, 'if she shoals out to twenty fathoms or less.'

'Right, sir,' the bos'n grunted.

Joe went into his cabin and collapsed. Twenty minutes

later he swung his feet out onto the cold linoleum and sat, chin in hands, on the edge of his bunk. What had he forgotten? They had food: they had water. Everything was going according to plan.

Slowly, he worked back over the last two days. Today was, or would have been, Saturday. He wondered what the Old Man and his visiting brass from the Bureau of Ships would have to say when the *Alice* was not in her proper slip with polished brightwork. The one good thing about time travel, Joe decided, was that he didn't have to worry about some admiral stumbling across Cookie's still. And there was that other business too:

When Ensign Joe Rate had shown up unexpectedly with a brand new commission in his hand, there had not been a single activity in the whole navy which actually needed a brand new ROTC ensign. Just when he had seemed doomed to a lifetime of awaiting orders, someone had remembered the *Alice*.

Commander Cutlott had been explicit. 'Those two pirates'—he referred to Gorson and Cook—'are prime contenders for the all-navy cumshaw and looting title.'

'Haven't they ever been caught?' Joe had asked in his innocence.

Commander Cutlott passed a weary hand over his bald spot. 'We're not dealing with amateurs,' he grunted. He leaned forward confidently. 'Things were bad enough when they confined themselves to supplies. How often do you find a team capable of stealing a whole ship?'

Joe's eyes widened.

'Yes,' Commander Cutlott sighed. 'Using a navy ship for their drunken parties—women aboard, no less!'

'Really, sir—' Joe began.

'Drunken, naked screaming women!' Commander Cutlott's voice was rising. 'Those god damned pirates have somehow managed to get the *Alice* asea with a full complement of whores. She's been sighted dozens of times. And yet, whenever I get down to the dock there she lies with those two freebooters scraping and painting, looking for all the world like Captain Mahan might have, if he'd managed to be born without Original Sin!' The commander's voice had risen a full octave and he was beginning to chant. 'Catch those two filibusters and I'll see you get another stripe.'

Even in an atomic navy promotion is neither immediate nor easy. Joe had left the commander's office with a foreboding of what he might get if he didn't catch them.

The linoleum in the *Alice's* cramped captain's cabin had numbed his bare feet. Disgustedly, he thrust himself back in bed and tried to sleep. He had nearly succeeded when abruptly he sat up, cracking his head on the bottom of the locker above. *The bow!*

Holy Appropriation! The *Alice* had rammed another ship two days ago and still no one had crawled into the bow to see if any of planking was sprung. He swung out of bed and grabbed a flashlight.

Galley and forecastle were dark. He picked his way through them without turning on lights, orientating himself by the gentle swish of water and not-so-gentle snores. The crawl hole between forecastle and chain locker was barely large enough to squeeze through. He stuffed the unlit flashlight into the waistband of his skivvy drawers and pushed himself through. After a moment's squirming over the jumbled anchor rope his hand touched warm flesh. He flinched backward.

The sleeper lashed out blindly. Something sharp grazed Joe's forehead. He cowered back, hands before his face to ward off another blow. There was a smack like a cleanly caught ball as a wrist slapped squarely into his palm. Joe caught it instinctively and jerked. He threw a right cross into the darkness. It missed and they wrestled in silent ferocity. He twisted the wrist until he sensed that the knife had fallen. He was scrabbling meanwhile with his free hand for a firmer grip. His forearm struck teeth which promptly bit him. He jabbed an elbow at them and eventually caught the other hand which still flailed.

Spreadeagled figures strained in a silent, horizontal waltz while he worked his knee between kicking legs and forced his weight onto the other. Though Joe had never regarded himself as an athlete, he was overpowering his assailant with surprising ease. The heels stopped kicking at his back, and he brought the spreadeagled arms cautiously together until he could rest his elbow on one and grip the other with the same hand. He felt about for the fallen flashlight and turned it on.

His attacker was Raquel.

He wondered momentarily why she had chose to sleep in the nude, but even in mid-surprise his first impression was of the perfect round firmness of her breasts. She glared at him and Joe became acutely aware that his skivvy drawers were not designed for modesty. Why did he have to be caught in these ungainly garments? Better to be honestly naked. He dropped the flash; its soft reflected light bathed her profile in a boudoir-like glow. She saw Joe's face for the first time.

The glare left her eyes, fading slowly into another emotion. Her lips were beginning to pout where he had elbowed. There were teethmarks in his forearm and a trickle of blood soaked his eyebrow.

Raquel no longer struggled. Joe realised abruptly what was expected of him. The sight of her was playing hob with his glandular system, but while he hesitated he sensed that the moment had passed.

Neither of them moved. Over their heads a sheep stamped and baa'd irrelevantly. Joe took his gaze from her and saw the knife. Stretching across her to reach for it, he

38

was conscious of flesh sliding over flesh, but then Raquel had wormed her way out from under him and was scrambling into one of the dresses she had used to floor the compartment.

He realised with sudden horror that someone could awaken at any minute. Or the deck watch could come below. This situation was bound to contribute little toward his dignity as master of the *Alice*. Still, there would be something definitely chicken-hearted about retreat.

He put on his most severe face and pointed down at the rope and chain which floored the compartment, then up at the eye where it threaded through the deck. 'If someone dropped anchor,' he said, 'you'd come up through that hole one shred at a time.'

Raquel did not understand the Twentieth Century word. '¿Ancla?' she asked.

'Ancôra,' Joe hissed. He hoped the Latin would get through to her. 'It goes down; you go up!' He made slicing motions and pointed at the chain. Suddenly Raquel understood and her eyes grew larger.

Joe remembered why he'd crawled into this hole. He shined the light around, looking for sprung seams. Tomorrow he'd have the chain tailed out so he could check the lower half of the locker. Meanwhile, he'd explored enough for honour's sake. Any moment now someone would wake up and peer through the open crawl hole.

'Don't let me catch you in here again,' he said severely, 'or I'll turn you into a pumpkin.' He tossed the knife into her lap and backed through the hole. He'd been in bed several minutes before he realised that he'd locked his door. He got up and unlocked with silent thanks that no one had come to wake him. Things like locked doors got men to shaking their heads whenever the Old Man's back was turned. He went back to bed again and, naturally, couldn't sleep.

He realised he'd been taking a lot about the girl for granted. With a knife and a disposition like that perhaps even the Vikings had respected her privacy. But if she was such a scrapper, what had been going on up in the bow last night?

3

Light glowed down the crack of his door. Joe looked out and saw Freedy at the fathometer. 'Sixty fathoms,' the radioman said. 'Cut yourself?'

'Bumped a stanchion,' Joe said. He touched the scab on his forehead and went on deck. McGrath was at the wheel.

'Day, Mr. Rate,' he asked, 'are you sure this's only nine hundred and something?'

Joe shrugged and admitted to himself that he'd only half believed it up till now. *Holy Neptune, what a thesis I could write on the Vikings!* 'I'm afraid it's true,' he said.

McGrath muttered something about God. Joe looked at him. 'I don't believe He would let it happen,' McGrath said.

Joe didn't know what to say to that, so he said nothing.

After a minute of two McGrath said, 'Funny—if it were true I'd be the only Christian in the world.'

'It's only a thousand A.D.,' Joe protested. 'Not B.C.'

'I know,' Howie sighed. 'But Martin Luther wouldn't be born yet.'

Joe turned to hide his grin from the faint glow of the binnacle lamp. The grin threatened to become a belly laught so he went below.

The sun was an hour high when Gorson woke him. 'Bottom's shoaled out to eighteen fathoms,' the chief said. 'Are we going to pile into Ireland?'

Joe stuffed an arm into his oilskins and rushed up the ladder. Bucking steep seas under shortened sail, the *Alice* was making as much lee as headway. Freedy stuck his head out of the after scuttle. 'Ten fathoms,' he yelled.

A half hour passed, then suddenly a grey-green band was visible as they topped each swell. Joe studied the *Alice's* wake and knew they'd never weather it. 'Steady as she goes,' he said, and ducked below. As near as he could guess from the *Alice's* meagre charts, the land must be Erris Head. 10° W longitude ran straight through this northwest corner of Ireland, but if the wind held the *Alice* would have to run through it too.

They had hoped to make for uninhabited land but this weather was going to change their plans. Why, Joe wondered for the thousandth time, couldn't the U.S. Government afford a full suit of sails? He would have to put the men to sewing in reef points at the first opportunity. Oh well, he philosophised, if it weren't for some parsimonious clerk I might not be seeing Ireland. Funny, he thought, but we know more about Greece in 1500 B.C. than we know about Ireland even three thousand years later.

Gorson was studying the coastline. 'Nothing,' he said, passing the glasses to Joe.

Joe took his own look. 'There,' he said. 'Not much of a harbour but at least they aren't breaking. It's the only hole downwind so we haven't much choice.' He tried to remember what he knew about Ireland. The Norse controlled the east coast, he was sure, but western Ireland had managed to remain fairly free from Norse colonisation, he thought.

Then he saw the ships.

There were four of them—Viking ships, rowing straight into the wind. Joe guessed they intended to round Erris Head under oars, then drive down the Galway coast on a raid. At least, that had been their original intention. Now, as they sighted the *Alice* driving straight toward them, the Norse rested their oars and waited.

Joe looked around for the engineman. Rose was on deck, along with everybody else. 'Better light her off,' Joe said. Rose nodded and took a fresh bite on his cigar as he ducked down the scuttle.

The Vikings were less than three miles away. Men stood by the *Alice*, ready to take in sail the instant the engine started. 'What in hell's keeping Rose?' Joe asked.

Gorson came back a moment later. 'That fertilising stove!' he explained. 'When he cut it off the other day he got the valves crossed up and cut off the engine too.'

'Great!' Joe moaned. 'Better get out the rifle.' There was no hope of turning the *Alice* to tack out of the bay.

'He's working,' Gorson consoled. 'It'll be ready any minute now.'

Minutes passed and still no engine. He could lower sail but if he did the Vikings would only start rowing again and the *Alice* would be dead in the water. Better keep canvas on and try to crowd through them.

The gap closed to half a mile. The Vikings waited, spread evenly before the route the *Alice* would have to take. Joe took the wheel and bore steadily for the gap between the two middle ships. They were less than a hundred yards apart and he would be exposed to spears and darts from both sides. 'Everybody go below,' he said, 'except Cook. I want you here with the rifle.'

Joe and Cookie crouched in the foot-deep cockpit, waiting for the first spear to fly. The *Alice* floundered along, much more slowly than Joe had thought possible. The two centre ships were about seventy yards distant on either flank. They aren't even closing in, Joe thought.

The Norse could see that, although his rig was a trifle strange—from somewhere in Arab country by the looks of those crazy three cornered sails—she was not rigged for

43

rowing. Once around the headland she would have to moor or breech and they could finish her off at leisure.

The engine sputtered and caught. Joe waited a moment to see it it was going to keep running. The Vikings were a quarter mile behind them now and the *Alice* was nearing the turning point if she was going to moor in this bay. Heads peeped cautiously out of the fore and after scuttles.

'All clean,' Joe yelled. 'Come up and take a sail.' And what were the Norse going to think when they saw the *Alice* running dead into the wind without oars or sails?

The channel was narrower here and the Norse were following them in. The *Alice* turned and there was a scurry to go below again as men remembered the rain of spears from their first Viking. She was making her full ten knots now and Joe hoped the lightly built dragonships would not be eager to ram. He lay face up in the cockpit, steering with a foot on the wheel. Cookie rested the rifle over the cockpit coaming. They'd have to rig some kind of shelter over the cockpit if this was going to keep up.

A bearded giant threw the first spear. It thunked into the *Alice's* foredeck and stood thrilling. The rifle cracked and he crumpled. Joe glanced the other way and saw a longship racing in. They were going to ram after all!

Suddenly there was a keening wail. Raquel stood atop the after scuttle, making snakelike movements and shrilling something with a poetic rhythm. Abruptly, the Vikings sheered off, leaving the *Alice* to chug her placid way around Erris Head where she could set sail again. The girl disappeared below.

At least he had longitude. It galled Joe to think that this information had cost an hour's fuel. Red Schwartz relieved him at the wheel. 'Mr. Rate,' he asked, 'you know anything about doctoring?'

Something began to shrivel inside Joe's stomach. 'What's wrong?' he asked.

'Well, Howie ain't much for talking but he's been acting funny all day.'

'Howie?' Then Joe remembered: McGrath. 'I'll see what I can do,' he said, which he admitted to himself was practically nothing. He went below and drew a cup of coffee. The Bible spouter was stitching a reef point into the mains'l, along with everybody else. His thin, ascetic face seemed no more drawn than usual. Joe wondered if Schwartz were imagining things. Still, they were buddies. . . .

It rained that night and sheet lightning flashed about the horizon. Lightning had got them into this, Joe remembered; he wondered if another bolt could get them out. But the lightning came no nearer. He looked at the clock and decided it was time for another sight.

The deck watch was sitting in the galley. When Gorson saw him with the sextant he got up and followed Joe. They waited until a wave had passed over, then dashed up the scuttle. Gorson grabbed Joe about the waist as he wedged himself against the mizzen. At that moment the *Alice* essayed one of her more spectacular rolls and green water swirled over their heads. 'You all right?' Gorson yelled as they breathed air again.

'Yeah,' Joe shouted. 'Let's go below.'

'Aren't you gonna take a sight?'

'Can't. I just lost the damn sextant.'

Dr. Krom looked up when they came below. 'That was quick,' he said.

'Practice makes perfect,' Joe said absently. He shot a glance at Gorson and the chief followed him into the tiny cabin. Gorson's broad brow was screwed into thoughtful wrinkles.

He squinted shrewdly at Joe and said, 'You know, Skipper, I think I've finally figured the angle on this operation.'

45

'Oh?'

'It's one of those drills, isn't it? Like that thing the army's always pulling with a bunch of dogfaces in screwy uniforms sneaking around. You know—they let the air out of the C.O.'s tyres and slam everybody in the brig to prove the whole lashup's not paying attention. It *is* just a drill, isn't it?' He said grinning.

'Nobody told me,' Joe grunted. 'If it is, I'd like to know how they doctored up the whole damn ocean.'

The glint went out of Gorson's eyes. 'Yeah,' he said glumly, 'they wouldn't kill that many guys unless it was for real.' There was a long pause. 'So what do we do now without a sextant?' he finally asked.

Joe shrugged. 'Sailors got by for four thousand years without them.' *But I didn't,* he added to himself.

'Gonna tell them?' The chief gestured toward the galley.

'They have enough worries now.'

'I hope you know what you're doing.'

'Have you any ideas?'

The bos'n looked at Joe for a long half minute. 'No sir,' he finally said. 'You're the captain.'

So I am, as long as they believe in me. And now if I believed . . .

They went back into the galley and Joe drew a cup of coffee. 'Cookie, did you wash your socks in this?' he sputtered.

Cookie looked hurt. ''Tain't much as coffee goes but it ain't bad for burnt rye.'

'Ah wish we had some chicory,' Guilbeau added.

'Joe looked at him.

'We just about outa coffee,' the Cajun said.

Joe sighed and took another sip. He was trying to drink it when Raquel came to sit beside him. 'Forgive me,' she said. 'I wouldn't have used the knife if I'd known it was you.'

Joe thought this over for a moment and decided he didn't

46

have an answer. Instead, he asked, 'What did you say to those Vikings?'

'I told them you would . . .' The rest trailed off into something Joe couldn't understand. She repeated it and he learned that he was a sorcerer who could call down lightning. Raquel was silent for a moment. 'By the way,' she finally said, 'who are you?'

Joe put his cup down. She was not, he realised, going to be fubbed off with any Great White Father routine. She nodded at Villegas who played poker with Schwartz and Freedy. 'The dark one hailed in my language,' she explained. 'I thought you were of my people.'

'How much has Villegas told you?'

She shrugged. 'He is foolish and thinks only of love.'

'I haven't observed him pestering you much.'

'I told him I belonged to you and that you would be angry.'

'Oh my God!' Joe moaned. He took another sip of bitter rye and thought of the inevitable Board of Inquiry he would someday face.

'He says women vote,' Raquel continued.

Joe waited.

'What does vote mean?'

Joe explained briefly about elections.

'So the women choose your prince and banish him if times do not prosper?'

'Well . . .' Joe began.

'Did women make you captain?'

'Not intentionally,' Joe said, remembering Ariadne Battlement. 'Where did you come from?' he asked.

She said something and he caught Burgos. He nodded absently, his mind on the new noise which had suddenly added itself to the *Alice's* creakings and groanings. It was a rhythmic clank-bang as if a piece of chain was sweeping across the wet deck. Wearily, he buttoned his oilskins and started up the ladder. Just as he opened the hatch it stopped. *To hell with it,* he thought, and came back down to the galley. Raquel still sat where he had left her. 'But Burgos is over a hundred miles from the sea,' he said, suddenly remembering. 'How did Vikings catch you?'

She nodded and started to explain. The noise started again. Joe put his fingers to his lips. The noise didn't seem to be on deck after all. He crept forward with a hand to his ear. It stopped again. A weakened chain plate could dismast them. But it sounded too far forward for that. Maybe the anchor chain was rattling in its chock.

'When I was eight,' Raquel continued, 'my father took me to Santander.'

It started again. Joe waved an angry hand and crept forward. In the forecastle Cookie held a stick of firewood with a hole drilled through it. One end of the copper coil from their homemade still projected through the hole. While sheep crowded around observing interestedly, Gorson was trying to flame the tube with a mallet and marlinspike.

Relief gushed through Joe and culminated in a whirlpool somewhere beneath his stomach. 'Damn it!' he yelled. 'Haven't we got enough trouble without you playing junior scientist?' And what was the forecastle going to smell like by morning? But . . . the sheep couldn't stay on deck in this weather.

'Well hell, sir,' Cookie began, 'we was just gonna make some rye whiskey.'

'You'll make salt water taffy if I catch you screwing around with that thing again. Where d'you think our next load of food's coming from?' He turned and stamped out of the forecastle. Back in the galley he absently drew another cup of burnt rye. Raquel still sat at the table. 'Now what were you saying?' he asked.

'Oh go listen to your noises!' she flared, and ran out of the galley.

Now what got into her? Joe wondered. *And what's*

48

gotten into me? He would never again have an opportunity to study this period. What would Dr. Battlement have given to question a citizen of medieval Spain firsthand? But then, she was a woman and therefore uneducated. A peasant too, which cubed her ignorance. He could probably get more from a world almanac than he would ever extract from Raquel about her own neighbourhood. It would be nice to cross paths with an educated man of this era, but there was little chance of that. Besides, he had to take the crew to the Azores and figure this mess out. 'To hell with history,' he muttered, and went to bed.

Light glowed down the edge of his door and switches snapped as Freedy checked the fathometer. The lights went out again. Had he been too sharp with Gorson and Cookie? Who ever heard of such a crazy idea for a vacuum still anyhow? A coil inside a bell jar! The copper spiral had looked like Dr. Frankenstein's patented mummy resurrector.

Holy Appropriation! The more he thought about it the more possible it seemed. Dr. Krom must be right after all: the *Alice* was the first ship ever to disappear into time. She was the first ship ever to have a screwy coil set at just the proper angle, with just the proper radius and spacing inside a partially evacuated bell jar—and at just the moment when a bolt of lightning had come along to power the apparatus. Gorson and Cookie's still was the time machine! He stopped fighting the idea and immediately slept.

It was still blowing like an Eskimo in Texas next morning. Cookie's pancakes had a leaden texture so he guessed Dr. Krom had gotten his mill to grinding rye. One problem solved; now, what about the navigation? Could he design an astrolabe? No, Joe decided. Maybe Columbus knew how to keep that silly little pendulum from swinging but Joe knew he'd never get an observation from the *Alice's* plunging deck. How about a cross staff? The trick was to hold

49

the long stick on your cheekbone and slide the T head until one end touched a star and the other was on the horizon. He sketched what he wanted on a paper towel and gave it to Abe Rose.

'What's wrong with the sextant?' the engineman asked.

There I go again, Joe thought. He hadn't expected Rose to know a cross staff from a ripsaw.

'I read a book once,' Rose added with a thin smile. 'But maybe I can fix the sextant.'

'What sextant?' Joe muttered. He went to look for Gorson and Cookie. They were in the galley, scowling into mugs of burnt rye. 'Where's Raquel?' Joe asked after a moment.

'Last I saw, she was looking for a quiet corner to slash her wrists.'

'Seasick?'

Gorson shook his head. 'What'd you chew *her* out about?'

'Why, I never said a word . . .'

'That explains it,' Cookie said.

'About the still,' Joe said after a long pause. 'Do you think you could get it working?'

Cookie's face lit up. 'Why shore,' he said. 'Just give me a couple of days to sour the mash.'

'I mean the way you were doing it before.'

Cookie was hurt. 'You don't like rye whiskey?'

'If I survive this cruise I'll never look a pumpernickel in the face again.'

'We ain't got any dried apples left,' Cookie protested.

'I'm not interested in booze,' Joe said patiently. 'I just want it set up the way it was when lightning struck.'

'An idea?' Gorson asked.

'I'm not sure, but we'll have to start somewhere.'

'Cain't,' Cookie said.

Joe looked at him.

'The bell jar. Hit busted in a million pieces.'

Joe sighed and took a breath. 'Rose!' he shouted.

The engineman popped his round face into the galley. 'It's not quite ready,' he said.

'Forget the cross staff for a while. Do you have any of those 5 gallon bottles that Krom's distilled water came in?'

Rose mouthed his cigar. 'I think so,' he said.

'We need a bell jar.'

The engineman grunted and disappeared.

The *Alice* drove southward through eight more days of heavy weather before the still was assembled and ready. The water bottles's corked neck had been dipped in paraffin. It's bottom, snapped off where Rose had flamed a gasoline soaked string, was not perfectly flat. After abortive experiments with lengths of split rubber hose, Cookie had sealed it with a gasket of dough.

All hands stood by in anxious silence as Gorson humped over the vacuum pump. Joe glanced from him to Cookie. 'You're sure everything's just the way it was the first time?' he asked.

'Yes sir,' Cookie said.

'What now?' Gorson asked.

'Keep everything ready and wait for lightning.'

Another day passed before Gorson called him from his bunk. 'Line squall building up,' the chief said. 'Who's gonna steer?'

'I am,' Joe said.

'You're the only guy can navigate this bucket,' the bos'n protested.

'It's my idea so I take the risks.'

'But you can't just . . .'

'Like hell I can't.' Joe went on deck. Villegas was steering and Guilbeau was on forward lookout. They tied him to the binnacle and went below. The scud of black cloud was barely two miles away. Forks of lightning danced in its depths. The wind died and in the abrupt calm Joe heard thunder. An immense anvil-headed cloud bore toward the *Alice*.

The calm was abruptly shattered by a tremendous gust which knocked the yawl on her beam ends. Wind wailed as the *Alice,* taking every third one over the bows, tore along with her cockpit filled. Joe took a deep breath and wondred when he would learn to fasten the top button of his oilskins. An avalanche of green water engulfed him and the yawl shuddered. After a long moment he gulped air again and twisted his head, feeling for the wind. The *Alice* was three points off and still turning. He spun the wheel with a silent prayer to Mahan's ghost.

Lightning struck.

4

The next thing Joe felt was Gorson forcing a vile taste into his mouth. The squall had passed and the *Alice* raced along under single reefed main. Here and there patches of blue peeped through the clouds. 'Did we make it back to our own time?' Joe asked.

'Dunno,' Gorson said, 'but I doubt it.' He gestured astern.

They weren't Vikings. The towering sails had a faint Arabic look. One thing Joe was sure of: he'd know more soon. Even as he looked the strange fleet gained on the *Alice*.

He tried to stand up. Panic flashed through him as muscles refused to obey; the lower half of his body felt asleep. Cold sweat gushed and ran in little trickles inside his oilskins. He took a deep breath and strained again. He felt nothing. Then he saw his foot move and knew he was not permanently damaged. Little by little, he felt control and feeling return. 'Better let us take you below,' Gorson was saying.

'Below, hell!' Joe snapped. 'I'm still captain of this ship. I want to know what the lightning's done to her this time.'

The standing rigging still good. Cookie appeared from nowhere. 'Nothing happened to the still,' he said. Joe tried again and found he could sit up. His legs itched horribly and he fought the impulse to scratch.

Dr. Krom swam into his narrowed vision. 'Are they friendly?' the old man asked, glancing back at the ships.

How should I know? But captains and gods were expected to know all things. 'Judging from this century's past performance, I'd say we didn't have a friend in the world,' he said.

Raquel was crowding up. *She's worried about me,* Joe thought. Why should she worry over an invincible god? The look of tender concern she wore made him almost forget what she had done to the Norse women. She studied the fleet which pursued them. 'Do you recognise them?' Joe asked.

'*Moors,*' she said.

He wondered what Moors were doing this far north—but the real question, he realised, was just how far north they *were*. The cross staff had conned him into believing he was off Portugal, but if it were spring instead of late summer, with days getting longer instead of shorter, he could be wrong—wrong enough to tangle with a fleet coming back from the Slave Coast.

They were driving east, probably into the Mediterranean. Moors were supposed to be more sophisticated than their Christian neighbours but Joe doubted if their civilisation had progressed to the point of respecting an unknown flag. The high lateen rigs bore an amazing resemblance to ships he had seen in Indian Ocean travelogues and would, he suspected, beat very handily to windward. Anyhow, they were too well spread out for the *Alice* to pull something fancy like circling behind them to gain the weather gauge.

Schwartz and Villegas were already hoisting the spinnaker up on deck. If they could gain headway the *Alice* might slant off and try to lose them. Maybe the Arabs wouldn't search too hard for one small and not very profitable looking ship.

Under all sail, they skated on half-mile sleighrides down

following seas. Stays thummed and all hands watched nervously, wondering how soon the spinnaker would blow out.

Two hours passed and it was still in its boltropes. The Moors should have been well behind by now—instead, they were gaining. Joe studied the leading ship in his binoculars. Swarthy, ragheaded men with satanic beards stared back with equal interest. He thought wistfully of the engine but the *Alice* was already over her natural speed. The engine would slow her down.

Raquel appeared beside him. 'What do you know about them?' Joe asked. Her tirade was too fast for him to follow but the meaning was clear. They held half of Spain in the Tenth Century. 'Do you speak their language?' Raquel shook her head. 'Perhaps they'll understand yours?' Clearly, she was not interested.

'Why do you wait?' she asked.

Joe gave her a look of bleak inquiry.

'When will you call down lightning?'

Gorson joined them in the stern. 'What's she saying?' he asked. Joe translated, wondering if all gods were troubled thus with unreasonable demands from their worshippers. There was a moment of silence as Gorson picked his teeth. 'I don't think it'll work,' he finally said.

'Nor do I,' Joe agreed, 'but we can give it the old college try. How many flares are left?'

'I'll go see.'

'Are they real Arabs?' McGrath asked.

Joe was about to explain that they were Moors when he realised the god shouter wouldn't know the difference. 'Here's your chance to kill a few Infidels and rescue the Holy Sepulchre,' he said.

McGrath stared at him.

'Either we win our own little crusade or we're liable to be converted.'

'Converted?'

'Would you rather be a live Moslem of a dead Christian?'

'What's a Moslem?'

'A Mohammedan,' Joe explained.

Gorson came back. 'Eleven flares,' he said.

Cook appeared with the rifle. 'Ninety-one rounds,' he reported, 'but I think we gonna need more'n that.' Joe had nearly a box of pistol ammo. Kill a man with each shot and we'll take care of two ships, he thought. Just find a way to clobber the other twelve and we've got it made.

Dr. Krom and his seasick assistant appeared. 'Do you think they'll attack?' Lapham asked.

'Of course not,' Gorson growled. 'As soon's they see our papers they'll apologise for bothering us.'

The effects of the lightning were nearly worn off and Joe was thinking in high gear again. 'Get Rose,' he said. Lapham went below and returned in a moment with the engineman. 'How long would it take to string some bare wire around the gunwale?' Joe asked.

'Well bless my bacon, cried the rabbi.'

Joe stared at the usually dour engineman.

'My uncle's a Zionist,' Rose laughed. 'He'd get as big a charge as they're going to if he knew I was about to fry some Ayrabs.'

'How big will it be?'

'Two kilowatts ought to take the curl out of their whiskers.'

Joe remembered their last brush with the Norse off Ireland. 'Will we be having any last minute engine failures?'

'If we do I'll cut my throat,' Rose promised.

And ours too, Joe thought.

'What will you use for wire?' Dr. Krom asked.

'The input transformer from your Christmas tree.'

'No!' the old man screamed. 'Half of my appropriation went into that . . .' Abruptly, he remembered where he was. 'I'll show them how to get it apart,' he said quietly.

Gorson and Cookie were already lashing sticks of firewood to the *Alice's* stanchions. Not bad, as long as they

56

stayed dry. If green water came over the rail something would blow up anyway. If it worked they could dream up something permanent. The Moors gained another quarter mile while Joe was thinking. Not the slightest chance of holding out until dark now. *To hell with all this running,* Joe thought. He was ready to meet the Tenth Century on its own terms.

Wires were soon strung and there was time to bring the dinghy aft. With it lashed to the boom crutch the steersman's back was protected from arrows or whatever the Moors would throw. Joe studied the arrangement and had mattresses lashed to the dinghy sides.

The leading Moor was only a mile away. Joe counted a fifteenth sail just coming over the horizon. 'We're ready, for once,' he said. 'When they come in range we'll try a couple of flares to put the fear of Allah in them. Maybe we can set fire to their sails. When they come close I want everybody below. I'll be protected at the wheel and I don't want any sightseers getting hurt. They may have slingers aboard, so keep the portholes shut.'

The leading ship was two hundred yards away, coming up slowly on the portside. 'Another fifty yards and they'll start throwing things,' Gorson muttered.

Joe rested the gun on the taffrail and took careful aim a hundred feet above the towering lateen sail. There was a pop and hissing roar as the flare curved in an arc which seemed sure to connect. The sail was white—linen or possibly cotton. Joe hoped it would burn. But the parachute opened too soon.

The flare floated gently into the water a few feet behind the speeding felucca. Impressive as it might have been in northern twilight, the blazing pinpoint was considerably less than lightning-size in bright afternoon.

'Another good idea shot to hell,' Gorson mumbled.

Joe handed him the flare pistol. 'Go below,' he said. 'Things may get a little hairy now.' He wasn't really worried though. He hadn't expected much of the flares. Thank Neptune the electric fence was ready. As he took the wheel he heard the generator start turning.

There was a twanging thunk as a catapult unwound on the *Moor's* foredeck. Something the size and shape of a garbage can sailed in a high trajectory toward the *Alice* and Joe knew with a sick certainty that if a stone of this size struck squarely it would go nonstop through deck and keel.

The missile struck amidships, shattering a portside stanchion. As fragments crunched across the deck Joe saw it had been a lage clay pot. The hot wire from the broken stanchion was dangling overboard. Over-loaded generators screamed and a smell of burning insulation came from below decks. And that, Joe knew, was the end of the electric fence.

The broken pot was sending up blue flames and clouds of stinking, sulphurous smoke.

Great Mahan's ghost! The slightest whiff of flame will melt that nylon spinnaker sheet in less than—Fluttering slowly like a manta ray, the spinnaker rolled forward and wrapped itself over the bow. Joe struggled to keep the yawl on course as she lost speed.

Gorson had a bucket and was sloshing water at the firepot. There was a warning creak and the mainsheet started running through its blocks. Joe threw the wheel hard aport, hoping he could spill wind before the boom came around and wiped out the standing rigging. Men came boiling out of the scuttle to fight the fire. Smoke blew aft as the yawl slowly turned. There must be unslaked lime mixed with it, Joe decided, for even under water the firepot burned.

From the corner of his eye Joe saw the *Moor* was also turning. Wind spilled from the huge lateen and both ships lost way. The felucca drifted towards them. They had the fire nearly out before a grapnel whizzed and thunked into the *Alice's* cabintop. A moment later ragheaded men

58

with Mephistophelean beards swarmed over the yawl's decks.

And the most amazing part of it was that nobody was hurt. An immense Negro with pointed teeth was tickling Joe with the tip of a yataghan before he had time to remember his pistol. Joe's happiness at being alive was tempered by the knowledge that he was cast in a mould of less than John Paul Jones' proportions. *They counted on me to see them through. What must they think of their captain now?* The *Alice's* men were lined up on deck, stunned and unbelieving. What will happen to Raquel? Joe wondered.

With the deck secured, several ragheads ventured below. Minutes of tense silence passed, then a Moor stuck his head out of the forward scuttle and shouted. A moment later someone in a more elegant burnoose and a turban several shades whiter leapt the breach between the felucca and the *Alice*.

Clean Turban had a widow's peak showing under his turban. His beard shone black and curly; it was trimmed very short and came to a neat point. Just like a Nineteenth Century portrait of Satan, Joe thought. The Moor looked at the *Alice's* men contemptuously and asked something in raucous Arabic. When no one answered he tried another language.

'I'm captain,' Joe said in English. The Moor didn't understand but he got his attention. It occurred to Joe that Arabs of this period studied Aristotle. He tried to remember some Greek. '*Egó imi keleustes.*' No, damn it!—that meant oarsmaster. What did he want to say? '*Navarchos.*' But there was no sign of understanding. '*Magister,*' Joe essayed. Maybe this joker knew Latin. Again it was no soap. He tried Raquel's Tenth Century Spanish and light dawned in the Moor's eyes. '*¿Christiano?*' he asked. The Moor pronounced it with a *kh* sound like the Greek *Chi*.

'Some of us are.'

'What land?' 'América.'

The Moor frowned. '¿Almeria?' he asked.

Joe shook his head. 'It lies west of here.'

'I have heard of this land,' the Moor said thoughtfully. 'But the people are savage with hair like a black horse's tail. What do you here?'

'Blown off course. Our food is nearly gone.' *Might as well get in a line about how little loot we have to offer.*

'Why did you throw fire at us?'

'Isn't that obvious?'

The Moor shrugged.

'Where are you heading?' Joe asked.

'Málaga. Our cargo sells at Granada.'

'Black men?'

The Moor nodded.

'You've taken care not to kill us. What will you do with us?'

The slave trader shrugged again. 'Isn't that obvious? Your ship is strange,' he reflected. 'Still, it'll bring more money than the lot of you.' He frowned at the *Alice's* crew. 'How many did you lose?'

Joe puzzled for a moment, then saw what the Moor was driving at. 'I lost no men.'

'It would take twenty hands to hoist the mains'l alone,' the Moor said contemptuously, 'and Allah only knows how many to set that which blew away.'

'Of your men, yes,' Joe agreed. 'But we have . . .' He was about to say magic when he realised that an Allah fearing Moslem might decide magicians were better off dead. 'We're skilled sailors,' Joe amended. 'Our ways are different.'

Clean Turban stroked the underside of his beard. Joe tried to guess what was on his mind. The Moor couldn't understand how the yawl sailed. His felucca was a mankiller with no winches and only primitive blocks in her rigging. She'd probably lost a few men on the run up from the Slave Coast. With a load of unbroken Negroes, Clean Turban needed every man for safety. Other ships were drawing up now but he had no intention of sharing his prize. He waved them angrily on. 'What weapons have you?' he asked.

'None,' Joe lied. He was acutely aware of the pistol in his belt. Thank Neptune he hadn't used it or they might all be dead. Why hadn't he been searched? Perhaps because no one aboard the *Alice* wore a sword or dagger and pockets hadn't been invented yet. He glanced at the crew and counted his meagre blessings.

The Moor was going to wonder about the pistol soon unless Joe drew his attention elsewhere. He took the binoculars from around his neck.

'What is that?' Clean Turban demanded.

'A gift which Allah has favoured us. I must evoke the Hundredth Name and then you shall see.'

Holding the binoculars before him like a chalice, Joe bowed and chanted:

> 'These boys never saw a pocket.
> Keep your hands at attention
> Or the jig is up.
> Amen.'

'Amen,' Clean Turban responded.

'Amen,' Cook and Guilbeau chorused.

'If you are among the blessed you will see. But there is danger here. Do you face Mecca five times daily?'

Clean Turban nodded.

'Do you fast on the appointed days?'

'Certainly.'

'Have you eaten the flesh of unclean animals?'

Clean Turban shook his head.

'Have you lusted after pagan women?'

The Moor hesitated a moment before answering.

'You may catch a glimpse of the Prophet's throne in Paradise. But if there is falsehood and evil in your heart . . .' Joe paused dramatically. '. . . Then Allah will strike you blind.' He fiddled surreptitiously until the binoculars

61

were out of focus and handed them over. Clean Turban put them clumsily to his eyes. 'I see nothing,' he said.

'You are not looking toward Heaven,' Joe explained. He pointed up and the Moor turned. Eventually, with Joe's help, he lined up on the sun and dropped the glasses with an ululating howl. Joe caught the strap and swung them back over his own neck. 'See,' he said comfortingly, 'you are not such an evil man after all. Allah has only warned you. You are not blind, are you?'

Clean Turban blinked tears and released a shuddering sigh of relief. 'Truly,' he said, 'you are men of the One God.' He turned and shouted instructions. Moments later a bent old man with scanty white beard was handed over to the *Alice* along with several prayer rugs and bundles. The boarding party started going back aboard the felucca. 'The *imam* and I will travel with you,' Clean Turban said, 'along with ten men-at-arms.' Which was not exactly what Joe had hoped for, but it was better than being murdered.

'All right,' he shouted, 'turn to and remember to keep those hands out of your pockets.'

Gorson started wrapping a long splice into the main-sheet while the others, realising that even under new management the ship had to be worked, went forward to take in sodden pieces of spinnaker. With patience and a great deal of stitching something might be salvaged.

Something else had been bothering Joe: Raquel was no-where in sight. He looked around the deck again and his suspicion was confirmed. Not only was the girl missing—so was Howard McGrath.

An hour passed before Gorson rove the mainsheet. The hindmost of the slavers was nearly abreast. With a little luck, Joe thought, they might dawdle behind until there were only the twelve men aboard to deal with. The prize crew had marvelled over blocks and sheeting winches. The yawl's wheel was a mystery for men had known only tillers but a young man, apparently son or nephew to Clean Turban,

62

took it. After a few spins and one near jibe he steered without difficulty.

Joe and Clean Turban faced each other across the galley table. Dr. Krom sat in a corner and surveyed the aged *imam* across the gulf of no common language. They had guided Clean Turban and the *imam* on tour of the electronic gear and had, with Freedy's collusion, managed to give the Moor a shock here and there to discourage meddling.

'What's that?' the Moor wanted to know. He was pointing at the vacuum still. Joe gave some fanciful explanation, only half paying attention to what he was saying. As carefully as possible he had searched for Raquel and McGrath. He wanted to ask if anyone had gone overboard in the mêlée but that would give them away for sure. Clean Turban and his men had been suprisingly decent so far. Prolonged conversations in English might change their attitude.

He still had the pistol stuck in his belt. He could perforate Clean Turban and the *imam* point blank, but there weren't shots enough to take care of all the guards.

Clean Turban was looking thoughtfully at Joe. 'Didn't you say you had no weapons?' he asked.

Joe held his breath. The pistol seemed to swell in his belt until it assumed the proportions of a rocket launcher. 'We are peaceable men,' he said. 'Pirates are unknown in our waters.'

Clean Turban smiled evilly. 'And yet you throw fire?'

Joe gave a cracked laugh. 'It's not a weapon,' he explained. 'We use the flares for signalling.' *How many left? To hell with them; sacrifice anything to relieve Clean Turban's mind.* He got the flare pistol and explained its workings. Clean Turban was doubtful until Joe explained what a parachute was and why it held the flare up.

The *imam* said something in Arabic and Joe suddenly wondered if he understood Spanish. If he did Joe might be on thin theological ice. Some kind of miracle which didn't set well with the Koran could easily get the lot of them axed for sorcery.

'You're traders,' Clean Turban said, 'yet I see no stock. What do you sell?'

Oh, what a tangled web we weave. Seconds passed and still Joe could think of no answer. After this stall it had better be good! 'A rare commodity,' he finally said. 'More precious than gold or ivory, worth more than silk or pepper. Our stock weighs nothing and takes no space in our ship. Yet it is worth more than the finest oils of Macassar.'

Clean Turban looked at him with a light, cynical smile. 'What can possibly be so precious?' he asked.

Joe smiled back at him and answered, 'Knowledge.'

When an avalanche of Infidels swept across the *Alice's* deck one quick look was sufficient for Howard McGrath. Joe's warning about crusades had made the situation woefully clear to Howie—and he wasn't very interested in dying at this moment. There was great commotion on deck, footsteps and much shouting in the Devil's tongue. Below decks, Howie raced about frantically. The chain locker was too open and obvious. Besides, that murdering heretic of a girl had her clothing in there and if he had to touch it Howie knew he could be sick.

He scurried through the ship, searching for a hiding place. Captain's quarters would be the first place they'd look . Lazarette? Full of rye and there wasn't room. Rushing to look for another place, he stumbled on the cabin sole. Rose must have been working on the engine, for the linoleum covered floorboard was slightly out of place. There was, Howie remembered, barely room to stretch out alongside the engine.

He kicked the floorboard over a little farther and dived. Abe must've had a mattress down here while he worked, for the landing was soft. Too dark to see for sure. Then inexplicably, the mattress snarled and sat up to jerk the floorboard back in place over their heads.

Howie's flesh crawled. His whole being wanted to erupt and run shrieking from this den of iniquity. Not enough to be penned in darkness with a murdering pagan. On top of it all she had to go and be a woman!

What would his mother say? But Howie faced the dreadful choice between should and must, for the footsteps were below decks now. Directly over his head someone was shouting in Satan's tongue. With Death standing over him and Eternal Damnation wedged tightly beside, there was only one thing left: Howie fainted.

The captain of the *Alice* had no time for such luxuries. Clean Turban was apparently satisfied with his cock and bull yarn about a Point Four programme, but it was chow time. The Moors wouldn't eat off plates. Cook finally put half the sheep in a dishpan and passed it up on deck with a few loaves of bread. 'Fewer dishes to wash,' he philosophised. Joe couldn't remember whether Tenth Century Arabs drank coffee. After a taste, Clean Turban's men passed up the burnt rye brew in favour of water. They sat around the dishpan, digging in with right hands, and emitting volcanic belches after each mouthful. 'I'll get some bicarb,' Cookie offered. 'When do we jump 'em?' he added under his breath.

'They like your cooking,' Joe explained. 'They're being polite.' He tried to throw in a mysterious smile in answer to the second question.

The *Alice* had been built with accommodation for ten. With Krom and Lapham aboard she carried twelve—Raquel made thirteen. Clean Turban and his *imam* brought it up to fifteen. And then there were ten men-at-arms. But it turned out that the Moors did not care for bunks, so the *Alice's* men slept undisturbed. The weather was clearing and with the Moors standing watch it began to look as if the

Alice's crew might get a full night's sleep for once. Joe took a final turn around the deck and Gorson clutched his sleeve. 'What're we going to do now?' the chief demanded when he had pulled Joe behind the dinghy.

'I don't know,' Joe said. He was shocked at the sudden realisation that he hadn't been giving much thought to the matter of escape. 'Something will turn up,' he said comfortingly. Gorson grunted and disappeared.

Clean Turban's young relation was still at the wheel. He steered confidently by the wind, ignoring the binnacle in front of him.

'Do you know what that is?' Joe pointed at the compass. The steersman smiled and shook his head. Joe had started to explain about compasses until the young man said something in Arabic and shook his head again. This one, at least, didn't know Spanish. But he knew where he was going.

Joe sighed and headed for his cabin. He found the white bearded *imam* squatting on his bunk, peering with much interest into the pages of Bowditch's *Navigation*. 'Can you read it?' Joe asked.

'No,' the *imam* replied to Joe's surprise. The old man had given no indication of understanding Tenth Century Spanish. 'But the diagrams and numbers make me suspect its subject matter.'

Joe collapsed into the chair. Throughout the afternoon he had alternated between hope and despair. Now he knew the *imam* was going to accuse him of sorcery. The storm, the responsibility of command, the nights of interrupted sleep, all had led him past exhaustion. Was that why he had given up so easily? He wondered if he could have made a better fight of it and tortured himself with thoughts of all the things he might have done. He had saved their lives —most of them, anyhow. If McGrath and Raquel were alive it was only a matter of time before they'd be caught. And when they were, Clean Turban might be less inclined to trust him. The *imam* was still looking at him with peculiar intentness in his rheumy eyes.

'There is no joy in losing,' the old man said.

'How would you know?' Joe muttered.

The *imam* laughed a short hard cackle. 'Do you think I was born a holy man?' he asked.

Joe stared.

'You claim to be a stranger,' the old man continued. 'I don't read your language but your maps are detailed and, I suspect, somewhat better than our own.' He laughed dryly. 'Are you Moslem?'

'There are very few Moslem in our country,' Joe hedged.

'Christian?'

'I doubt it,' the young man sighed 'Three equals one always looked like unsound mathematics to me; I've never made much sense out of the Trinity.'

The *imam* smiled. 'Then you believe in one god who does not go about splitting himself into disconnected particles?'

Joe thought a moment. 'There was a Jew in our land whose name was . . .' In search for words he unthinkingly translated a proper name into its roots. 'One Stone spent a lifetime studying the nature of God. Before he died he left us the Unified Field Theory. It proved that everything was controlled by the same law and that there can be no exception to the Law. I believed this man.'

'I think,' the *imam* said slowly, 'that you are a Moslem.'

'Suppose I were,' Joe sighed, 'what would it gain me?'

'I was born on an island which your map calls Corfu.'

'You must've been Christian!' Joe exclaimed.

'Slave or free, we go on living,' the old man continued. 'I truly believed in the divinity of Christ and in the Holy Trinity.'

'What changed your mind?'

'I was fourteen when they took me from my father's sardine boat. I spent two years as a camel boy in Alexandria.

'No, I wan't mistreated. My master was a simple, devout man who prayed daily for my guidance and conversion. When he died I was willed to the mosque and there a *muadhdhin* taught me to read.

'Conversion . . .' He waved a scrawny hand and spat. 'I learned Arabic years before I could read my native Greek —which, incidentally, you pronounce very poorly. As a Christian I might still be drawing water and hewing wood. As it is, I've passed a pleasant and scholarly existence. God may judge me in the next life. Let Him do it in the knowledge that I made the best of this one.'

'You think I should turn Moslem?'

'What can you lose?'

'My men and my ship.'

'Already gone. But if you'll be circumcised and profess Islam I may be able to keep you together. As long as you're together, who knows?'

'Why do you tell me this?'

The *imam* stroked his scant white beard and shrugged. 'Two reasons. I had four wives and twenty-one sons, no counting how many daughters. It's hard to remember their faces. Age makes fools of us all. But with each year I remember one face more clearly.'

Joe looked a question at him.

'I remember an old woman who died in Corfu, never knowing what became of her son. I was an only child, you know.'

Joe was silent for a long moment. Suddenly and irrelevantly, he remembered Ariadne Battlement. The last he had heard she was knitting socks and turning collars for another Bright Young Man.

'Sidi Ferroush is a fool,' the *imam* said, 'but he is a kind fool.'

Joe boggled for a moment, then realised the *imam* referred to Clean Turban. 'What was the second reason?' he finally asked.

'I have seen perhaps a hundred books in my lifetime, but never any like yours. I would hear more of your land. Oh, yes,' he added parenthetically, 'do not use that thing you keep trying to hide in your belt. Things will turn out better than you expect.'

5

Howie came to in cramped darkness and immediately wished he could faint again. The engine was digging cruelly into his back but it bothered him not so much as the softer protuberances which rubbed against his front. He was facing the she-devil—that much he could tell even in darkness. And she also faced him. But why, oh merciful God, did they have to be jammed in here end to end?

He felt cautiously about, trying to move a fraction of an inch away and cringed when his hand touched forbidden fruit. But if the she-devil intended to seduce him her tactics were highly unorthodox. A knee came in violent contact with his nose. Minutes passed while he breathed through his mouth, waiting for the fountain to clot. He wanted to snuffle or blow but Satan's emissaries were talking right over his head.

All dead now, Howie thought, remembering his shipmates. They weren't true Christians but they were friends. Then abruptly he recognised Joe's voice speaking in an unknown tongue. He was alive! The young skipper was not a true Christian either but his quiet competence always made Howie think wistfully of the father he had never known. He felt better already. Mr. Rate had coped with everything so far—he would cope with this. But how soon?

The she-devil squirmed and Howie was reminded of their desperate position. He discovered that her dress had crawled higher than it had any business crawling. He tried to move away and again his hand contacted forbidden fruit, round and firm like half a melon. Again her knees jabbed at his clotted nose.

Howie fought his arms down past the she-devil's body until he could encircle her flailing legs. There was no room to retreat, so he advanced, squeezing with all his strength. Still she struggled. Knees pummelled his cheeks like calking mallets. The she-devil would not stop kneeing him! It was almost as if she didn't want him to touch her. There was only one move left: Howie bit.

His incisors met in a particularly tender place just above the kneecap and the flailing immediately stopped. She lay stiff, trembling slightly like a newly saddled filly. Howie moved a cautious hand. Maybe he could find that confounded skirt and pull it down.

But the farther his hand moved the more softly interesting things became. I won't pull it down just yet, Howie decided. If he was to fight the Devil it would be well to familiarise himself with the Devil's weapons.

The she-devil squirmed again, shifting position with a thoroughly delightful wriggle. Tingling fire passed through Howie's virgin loins. I'll move my hand just a little farther, he decided. At that instant sheet lightning flashed through his closed eyes. Sparks and pinwheels banked billiard-like round the inner corners of his skull and he gave a yelp of outraged surprise. It wasn't only his nose she'd smashed; it felt like the trecherous she-devil had bitten off the tip of his big toe! He froze, waiting for someone to tear up the floorboard and discover them, but after several minutes it appeared that no one had heard. There was a long, thoughtful silence while Howie dwelt on many things.

Even as Joe Rate, he came to the belated conclusion that this she-devil was less freewheeling than would appear at first glance. She had not, Howie suddenly realised, the slightest intention of seducing him. The knowledge left him shaken to the very core of his being, for if she were defending her virtue then Howie's wandering hand had sinned him into a very tight corner. How could he ever make amends to God and Mother for attempting to lead this fair flower astray?

Why, she could probably be led down paths of righteousness and become a true Christian! But that was beside the point. He had wronged this girl. There was but one way to make amends. He would marry her.

The thought shocked him but there was no avoiding it. Come to think of it, hadn't St. Paul suggested it was better to marry than to burn? Howie could no longer hide even from himself the ardour with which he burned. It would not be pure sacrifice on his part, he decided.

But if he were to marry this fair flower he must first save her from the Infidel. A wave of shame swept through Howie as he realised that his betrothed was witness to this shameful, rodentlike cowering in darkness. He felt the strength of God flowing into him. It was time to act. But what was he to do? Why was Mr. Rate taking so long?

Joe and the *imam* still faced each other across the minuscule cabin. 'What kind of weapon is it?' the *imam* asked.

Joe took the pistol reluctantly from his belt. 'Fire burns in a closed place,' he explained. 'The smoke pushes a piece of lead out of this tube.'

'Ingenious,' the old man said. 'How far will it throw?'

Joe thought a moment, trying to remember if the Arabs used yards. Probably not. He spread his arms wide and said, 'Fifty times this distance.' He tossed the pistol into the drawer below his bunk with a careless gesture.

The old man was impressed. 'I should like to visit your country.'

'So would I,' Joe added with a sad smile.

The *imam* grinned wolfishly. 'You can bamboozle Sidi Ferroush with yarns about a fair continent, but I have talked with a man who went there. It is a worthless land,

72

filled with howling savages and strange sicknesses. I do not think you were blown off course. Nor do I think you are lost. You have charts and you have bits of crystal ground Archimedes fashion. No.' The *imam* laughed his short hard cackle. 'I believe in God but I do not see Paradise through a burning glass.'

Joe realised dimly that he was not at his best with an open mouth but he couldn't get around to closing it.

'You do not come from the Worthless Continent,' the old man continued. 'Your ship and tools are too fine for savages. Besides, you look like Roumi—Europeans.

'If I were still young and believed in the fabulous kingdom of Prester John—But alas, I am old and a cynic. Yet, I would give the remaining years of my life to know from whence you come.'

'You'd never believe me,' Joe said.

'Probably not,' the old man conceded, 'but that will not make me stop listening.'

Joe took a deep breath and began. It was a garbled account, punctuated with skippings back and forth as he remembered details, interrupted often with fumblings for words Joe didn't know and ideas which had never existed in Tenth Century Spain.

In the last few days Joe had become more proficient in the language—really more of an uninflected Latin than Spanish. As he told his tale one corner of his mind reflected on how he was slipping into new pronunciation with vowel sounds all different from what he'd learned in school. Abruptly, he broke off and began chanting:

'*Arma virumque cano, Troiae qui primus ab oris Italiam, fato profugus, Laviniaque venit . . .*'

The *imam* looked at him with a slight, quizzical smile.

'So that's how it sounded!' Joe marvelled, his face lighting with the first and only love of his life. 'Latin's a dead language in our time, you know. We could only guess at how it sounded.

'Litora multum ille et terrîs iactatus et alto
vi superum saevae memorem Iunonis ob iram;
multa quoque et . . .'

He continued, rolling over Virgil's meter with rising confidence. 'No wonder the empress fainted the first time she heard it!'

'I begin,' the old man said, 'to believe your fantastic tale.'

Joe looked at him.

The old man began chanting in a regular, even meter and Joe listened, tormented by a feeling that he could almost understand. The old man stopped abruptly. 'It's changed from his day to mine,' he explained. 'But that's how I think he might have sung it.'

'Again!' Joe said with mounting excitement.

The *imam* repeated, and abruptly the harsh syllables fell into meaning for Joe. Tears started in his eyes as he remembered Dr. Battlement. How many years would Old Prof given to hear the *Iliad* in Homer's accents?

'I see you recognise it.'

Joe nodded, not trusting himself to speak.

The *imam* was silent for a moment. 'You have the advantage,' he finally said.

'How?'

'We are history—to be read in any book. You are the future which is read in no book.'

'I'm afraid I can tell you little,' Joe said. 'And I wonder if I should tell you anything. I might change the course of history and erase my own present.'

The *imam* shrugged. 'I will change no history. I am an old man with no hunger to gratify but curiosity.' He laughed his single cackle again. 'I doubt if I am important enough to be inscribed in the histories, so I won't ask the

74

date of my death. But you could tell me, I think, what were or will be the fates of Islam and Christendom.'

'That brings me to a problem which has plagued me since this whole thing began. What year is this?'

'376.'

The 376th year of the Hijra, Joe calculated, would bring it to about 998 A.D. 'What month?' he asked.

'The Arab month is lunar and wanders all over the seasons. At the moment I can't remember what it would be by the Greek Calendar.'

'Has the summer solstice passed yet?'

'Oh yes, 70 days ago.'

So it was late summer after all. Where, Joe wondered, had he slipped up in his navigation? He reached absently for a cigarette and belatedly realised he was violating his own order about hands out of pockets. Oh well, he philosophised, the old buzzard had seen through everything else he'd tried to pull. He lit it with a sidelong glance to see how the old *imam* would react to matches. The old man merely watched interestedly without comment. Joe offered him a cigarette but the old man waved it away with a typically Greek gesture. When the smoke drifted his way he coughed.

'A disgusting habit,' Joe conceded. 'Let's go on deck where the air's fresher.'

Dr. Krom and Lapham were sleeping on the settees in the darkened galley. The oceanographer stirred and muttered an angry phase in Hungarian. *He'll sleep better tomorrow,* Joe thought. *We'll all sleep better when I pass the word. With a little luck the imam can swing an appropriation and some back corner of the Alhambra for us to carry out a few experiments.* All they would have to do was keep Mr. Big happy with an invention once in a while—an improved hour glass or something fancy in the way of weapons. He wondered if he could manufacture a parachute flare out of pitch and sulphur and whatever else would be available.

75

'How many of your people understand this language?' Joe asked.

'Most of them were born in Spain,' the old man said.

They made their way up into the *Alice's* bows, picking their way past sleeping Moors. The helmsman and two huge Negroes who leaned on scimitars in the yawl's waist all greeted the old man respectfully. Joe sat on the anchor winch and the *imam* squatted on deck beside him. All sails were drawing in the starlit night and Joe's admiration for the Moorish helmsman increased. He took a final puff on his cigarette and began telling the old man what had happened in the world since 998.

Howie lay facing his betrothed in the darkness. The strength of God was with him but what was he to do? There was, he decided, but one thing. Mr. Rate had made it clear: Kill a few Infidels in your own private crusade. How else could he recover his tarnished honour or repair the damage his sinful, wandering hands had done?

Cautiously, he pushed up the floorboard and caught a glimpse of Dr. Krom's bushy white head on the settee. *Didn't even throw his body overboard,* Howie thought, but then the old oceanographer released a snore and he was forced into another rapid revision of his beliefs.

His betrothed hissed something and pulled the floorboard back down. If this marriage were to be successful, Howie decided, it was time for him to assert his authority. With unbounded confidence. Howie pushed the floorboard up again and climbed out. He motioned Raquel to stay down by the engine but she scrambled out to stand beside him.

They faced each other in the dim nightlight, wondering what next? They couldn't stand here forever. Howie decided. He tried the door to Mr. Rate's tiny cubicle, and found it empty. He drew Raquel in and bolted the door before turning on the light. Mr. Rate kept a pistol in here somewhere—the question was where? *I'll start with the top drawer*, he decided, and there it was on the first try!

The pistol was loaded. But there were hundreds of Arabs aboard and only six shots. He rummaged through the other drawers but couldn't find the extra ammunition. He had to act soon, for the strength of God was upon him and Howie had a feeling that if he waited too long it would leave him. Besides, he decided, the pistol was all wrong. The first shot would bring them all upon him. He needed a quieter weapon. 'Do you have a knife?' he whispered.

Raquel looked at him blankly.

Howie made a slicing motion across his throat and pointed at her. Light dawned in his betrothed's eyes. Her hand went inside her bodice in a lightning gesture and reappeared with a short, double edged blade. Howie held out his hand but she refused, shaking her head. He realised she was right. *If God sees fit to take me I can't leave her to a fate worse than death*. He put a finger to his lips and, after turning out the light, opened the door.

The galley was still quiet. He tiptoed forward to the drawer where Cookie kept a small paring knife, a French chef's knife, a boning knife, and a cleaver. He turned and bumped into Raquel. 'I told you to stay in the cabin,' he hissed, but again she refused to understand English.

Howie crept forward into the darkened forecastle and searched for the bunk above his empty rack. Red Schwartz awakened with a startled grunt which Howie stifled with a pillow. His eyes opened and saw Howie offering him the boning knife. Schwartz was instantly awake; he took the knife and swung his bare feet down onto the cabin sole without a word.

Howie held up the remaining knives in mute question. Schwartz put a hand over Arnie Cook's mouth and shook the gaunt Tennessean gently. Cookie sat upright, cracking his head on the upper bunk. Seeing his French knife and cleaver, he instantly picked the French knife. 'Where's Mr. Rate?' he whispered, but they didn't answer.

'What the bastardly . . .' Gorson erupted when they woke him. He tore hands away from his mouth. Then he saw the cleaver and shut up.

Howie and Schwartz headed for the forward scuttle as Gorson and Cookie tiptoed for the after ladder. Why, Howie wondered, didn't Satan's men bother to post a man below decks? This carelessness could only mean that God was on Howie's side. Gorson, pondering the same question, decided the Moors felt contempt for any men who would give up with as little fight as they had.

'. . . and then in 1571,' Joe continued, 'a coalition of Christian states put an end to Moslem expansion at the Battle of Lepanto.' He reached absently for another cigarette and reminded himself that he had less than a pack remaining.

'Yes,' the *imam* probed, 'and was Christendom then unified again?'

But Joe's sailor half was watching the faint flutter which had developed in the luff of the mains'l. He glanced back just in time to see the Moor steersman go flying overboard. Someone—it looked like little Guilbeau—had the wheel and was already pulling the *Alice* back on course.

There was no mistaking the meaning of that sight. Joe's muscles tensed, but instead of the adrenalin of battle he found guilt and shame coursing through him. He should have been leading this insurrection himself, instead of discussing history.

He turned, ready to throttle the old man, but the *imam* had also seen what happened and merely watched with a lively interest in his rheumy eyes. They stared at each other in silent surmise while Joe cursed his indecision. This was the enemy! He should throttle him and then have a go at those bescimitared Negroes who lounged in the waist.

While he fluttered in indecision one of the Negroes glanced aft and saw Guilbeau at the wheel. The Negro shouted a single questioning word and abruptly an ululating fiend charged him. Still staring, Joe realised that it was McGrath. The little god shouter plunged his knife twice into the African's midriff, then spun to the other who had finally awakened to danger and was swinging his scimitar.

Gorson and Cookie were moving forward now to cover little Howie. In the bow there was shouting and a confused mêlée as Moors awoke to struggle with the *Alice's* men who boiled up out of the forehatch.

Joe and the *imam* stood side by side watching the fracas. The scimitar was decending and Joe could see that Howie's brief moment of glory would end in a mercifully quick death before Gorson or Cookie could rescue him. Then the scimitar faltered and its well aimed stroke merely mangled the god shouter's ear. Raquel and her knife again!

Clean Turban was amidships now, shouting to rally his men. Few answered. Little Howie had disentangled himself from the Negroes who lay gasping their life out on the *Alice's* deck. Shaking his head, he cast a semi-circular sprinkle of blood and his wild eye fixed on the *imam*. 'In the name of Our Lord, Jesus Christ!' he screamed, and sprang to kill another Infidel.

Joe fought through layers of paralysis. 'No!' he shouted. 'No, Howie, not this one!'

But the strength of God was in Howie and he wasn't listening. Joe pushed the old man behind him and held up his hand. 'Halt, damn it!' he said, and realised how ridiculous he must look. Howie's glazed eyes still fixed on the *imam* as if he could go through Joe without seeing him. Intensely aware of his own disarmed state, Joe reached for the knife and felt its tip move across his cheek bone. Howie's hand lifted him clear of the deck without deflecting appreciably from its course toward the *imam*.

'No!' Joe yelled again. He whacked the heel of his free

hand across the back of Howie's neck. He swung twice more before the little steersman slumped to the deck. The old *imam* still watched with the same detached interest when a moment later something struck Joe from behind and he followed Howie's downward course.

When he came to Gorson was bending over him—a grinning Gorson whose ear was nearly as mangled as Howie's, and who dripped blood from a bash paralleling his collarbone. 'What happened?' Joe mumbled; then he remember the *imam*.

'All our people are alive,' Gorson said.

'And the Moors?'

Raquel crowded through the *Alice's* men. 'The *imam* lives,' she said. 'He told me he was born Christian.'

'How many others?' he asked.

'Two surrendered.'

Joe wondered if Clean Turban was among them. He caught sight of the *imam*. 'And Sidi Ferroush?' he asked.

The old man shook his head. 'The helmsman was his son. He preferred to die fighting.'

All's fair in love and war, Joe tried to tell himself, but he couldn't rid himself of the sickness within him. 'It was not of my doing,' he said, looking at the aged *imam*.

The old man's eyes glinted understanding. 'You are almost as poor a captain as I am a priest,' he said. 'But neither of us chose the rôle we play in God's little farce.'

With silent thanks that none of the *Alice's* men understood, Joe struggled to his feet and nearly collapsed again from the throbbing at the back of his head.

'Easy, sir,' Gorson was saying, so Joe allowed himself to be led below, wondering if his failure was as apparent to everyone else as it was to himself. Cookie handed him a cup. He drank and gasped.

'What is that?' he wheezed.

'You said it was all right to set up the still again,' Cookie said.

'Oh Jesus!' Joe moaned. What would Commander Cutlott have to say when they met again? He limped into his cubicle. Lying down didn't help any. The *Alice* was his again—through no effort of his own. The same problems faced them—only more so.

The Azores were now two hundred miles farther upwind, and there were four more mouths to eat up their groceries and drink their water. Unfriendly mouths at that. For all he knew, one of those Moors was boring holes in the *Alice's* bottom at this moment. Why couldn't he have stayed in Dr. Battlement's history department?

Abruptly he remembered the *Alice* was still heading east. Every hour on this course meant five hours beating back. After the yawl was hauled about, tacking southwest, he found Rose and asked how much oil was left.

'Maybe thirty-five hours,' the engineman said. Joe hoped they wouldn't be caught again on a lee shore.

Then he remembered Howie. He'd have to congratulate him or something, if he'd calmed down. With a sudden grin he reflected that the god shouter was the only man in the navy who rated the Crusader's Cross.

When Joe went below Gorson was drinking burnt rye in the galley, glaring at the *imam* and two Moors who accepted their fate with equanimity and squatted in the opposite corner of the galley.

'Chief,' Joe said, 'do you think McGrath rates a medal?'

Gorson choked and sputtered over his rye, then sobered. 'How'd you happen to pick him to spread the word?'

Joe didn't have an answer ready. *Lousy captain—not even a good liar*. The *imam* and Dr. Krom were both looking at him. Joe was too young to realise that age did not automatically bring omniscience. Nor did it occur to him that the *imam* didn't understand English and that Dr. Krom understood nothing.

'I didn't pick him,' Joe said in a lame voice. 'I was working a different angle. Had us set up for a laboratory and a little peace and quiet once we were safe in Granada. The mutiny was Howie's show.'

Gorson whistled. 'I guess he does rate a medal.'

McGrath stuck his head down the scuttle. 'Squall brewing,' he said. 'Might be lightning.'

'Cookie, hop it with the still.'

'Agin?' Cookie asked despairingly.

'We ain't gonna have any sails left if you keep steering into these squalls,' Gorson grumbled

'Shorten sail and heave to,' Joe decided. 'We'll all go below this time.' He passed a hand over his face and discovered someone had taped the cut made by Howie's knife.

Little Howie was very quiet. Halfway in shock, Joe guessed. He wondered if the little steersman remembered what he had done or realised that Joe had rabbit punched him. He looked carefully but the little man's eyes were blank. Nor did he flinch when Joe swabbed his mangled ear with merthiolate.

Raquel smelled clean for a change. 'For what is the red paint?' she finally asked.

'It heals wounds quicker.'

'Put some on his toe,' Raquel said.

The god shouter's big toe was swollen. A blue patch radiated from two indentations in his nail. Like teeth marks, Joe thought. The skin was unbroken though, so he didn't waste merthiolate.

'Here,' Raquel said, pulling her ankle length skirt up to expose her knee. Joe painted the odd shaped wound just above her kneecap. 'Looks like another bite,' he said.

'It is.'

Guilbeau stuck his head down the scuttle. 'Be heah any minute,' he said.

'Everything tied down topside?'

The Cajun nodded and swung down the ladder, dogging

the hatch behind him. Joe glanced forward where Gorson and Cookie fussed over the still. Gorson nodded. All hands crowded into the galley, waiting excitedly for what the lightning would bring. Not much, Joe feared—at least it hadn't the last time. Then another horrible thought struck him.

He hadn't been too sure of his position before this fracas with the Moors. Now, with all this driving east, how far was the African coast? Or the Spanish coast? 'Freedy,' he said, 'how about firing up the fathometer?' He went to his cubicle and looked at the pilot chart, wishing for the hundredth time it were some kind of a chart with proper soundings. Even a hundred fathom curve would help.

There was a thumming of rain. A sudden explosive blast knocked the *Alice* on her beam ends. Then the yawl righted itself and began facing up to the squall.

Cookie humped over the still while Gorson watched anxiously. 'Ninety-two fathoms,' Freedy called. He had to yell to make himself heard over the squall.

Abruptly, the bottom dropped out of creation. Books and papers floated off the chart table and hung in mid-air, just as Joe himself floated off his chair. The *Alice* wasn't even rolling—she was falling, straight down on an even keel. The fall ended abruptly with a tremendous crunching splash and myriad clatters as objects within the *Alice* once more sought their proper level. Joe settled back into his chair with a spine-shattering thump. The binoculars whizzed past his nose and landed on his lap.

Out in the galley the *imam* and Dr. Krom sat upright and ashen in one corner. Gorson and Cookie were looking dazedly at the still, whose bell jar was miraculously intact. Freedy puckered his tiny mouth and god-damned something while banging his fist against the fathometer. 'Ninety-two fathoms a minutes ago,' he grumbled. 'Now the damned thing reads sixteen.'

'Switch ranges,' Joe suggested. He was trying to get the

hatch open, but it wouldn't budge. Water trickled around its edges. Abruptly he realised it was struck from the weight of solid water on the other side. At least thirty seconds had passed since the smash, but the yawl was still under water!

He took a deep breath and reached for a cigarette. He was out of them—damn it! He looked cautiously around to see if anyone had noticed the dripping hatch. They were recovering from the jolt and beginning to wonder about the strange silence. There was neither sound nor feel of the sea. There was no doubt in Joe's mind now; the *Alice* was making like a submarine!

Water would be leaking through the deck openings into the chain locker and through the charlie noble, a steady trickle coming down the rudder post. If they were at any depth the valves in head and bilge pumps would rupture. No, he guessed, if they were that deep the hatch would be stove in.

He stared at it, afraid to call anybody else's attention lest the whole crew panic. Water trickled slowly around the hatch. Water trickled down Joe's forehead and a cold prickle oozed between his shoulder blades.

6

There was a sudden waterfall as the *Alice* broke the surface. Joe released a tremendous breath. He forced the hatch and clambered topside. In spite of everything the *Alice's* close reefed sails were intact. Everything was there except the bloodstains on deck—and the dinghy.

Joe peered hopelessly into the dark, overcast night. No sign of the small boat. They'd have to swim ashore if they ever got to the Azores.

'Secure the still,' he told Gorson. 'There won't be any more lightning tonight.'

Guilbeau took the wheel and they shook out a couple of reefs to speed the yawl southwest. The wind was veering now and she ran more freely. 'Steady as she goes,' Joe told Cajun and went below.

Freedy was still thumping and god damning the fathometer. 'No matter what I do, it reads sixteen,' he grumbled.

'We're probably over the steeple of the First Baptist Chursh of Atlantis,' Joe said. 'Wake me if it shoals out to eight.' Hoping he inspired more confidence than he felt, Joe shut himself in his cubicle and again studied the damnably insufficient pilot chart.

He must be close to Gibraltar—but was he north or south of it? Either way, he consoled himself, the *Alice's* southwest course would carry her clear of any land. He stretched out carefully on his bunk and tried to find some position where the back of his head wouldn't throb quite so badly. He had almost found it when someone knocked and opened the door. 'Eight fathoms,' Freedy reported.

Joe pushed past him and scrambled topside. Nudging a startled Guilbeau from the wheel he spun it and spilled wind. 'I've had enough thrills for one day,' he said. 'Drop anchor.'

While they took in sail and unlashed the anchor the *Alice* drifted another quarter mile. Just as the anchor chain started rattling she ran gently aground.

The next few minutes were somewhat chaotic. Joe went into a frenzy of sounding, looking for a shore with his feeble battered flashlight, asking Rose for the thirtieth time when he was going to get that anomalous engine started. Eventually it did and the *Alice* chugged sedately away for a couple of miles while Freedy tossed a lead and chanted soundings. When Joe thought they were in deep enough water he finally allowed the anchor to be dropped again.

So much more fuel gone.

Dawn was rosy fingered as a Homeric couplet. Joe glanced at his wrist. Should've bought a new watch long ago but sentiment attached him to this venerable relic. Get it cleaned again if he ever got back. He looked around the *Alice*. Two miles west of her anchorage, a small island jutted from the sea. Goats grazed on its sparse vegetation and the almost vertical shoreline was crisscrossed with their tracks. All hands stared at this unexpected miracle.

'We could use some meat,' Cookie suggested.

'Yes,' Joe said absently. 'But can we spare the bullets?'

'Another thought occurs,' Dr. Krom's pedantic voice injected.

'I know,' Joe said. 'Where there are goats there's water.'

'How do we get ashore without a dinghy—or even if we had one?' Gorson asked after studying the sheer cliff face.

They weighed anchor and the *Alice* ghosted along in the light morning air, tacking around a headland. Freedy stood in the bow tossing the headline since he no longer trusted the fathometer. 'Six fathoms,' he chanted. 'Five and a half . . . seven . . . nine . . . no bottom at ten.'

They had passed over some ridges. Joe studied the island's contours and tried to guess which way they would continue under water. 'There it is!' Gorson shouted.

The yawl ghosted on to the southeast side where the crater opened, offering a perfect horseshoe inlet. A tiny rock pinnacle extended from its centre, like a lopsided pencil point. The harbour was perhaps two hundred yards across and here on the island's inner surface goats had not wrought as much havoc with the vegetation. Tiny patches of green showed between rocks. One rift in the crater wall had eroded into a canyon lined with scrub oak.

'No bottom at ten,' Freedy called again.

'How we gonna anchor?' Gorson asked. 'Wind shifts south and we've had it.'

'Perhaps,' Joe said. He took the wheel and headed the *Alice* toward the pinnacle. Throwing it hard left, he spilled wind and lost speed so that the yawl's bow drifted by within jumping distance. Grooves in the rock hinted that other mariners had tied up here.

Joe stripped to his skivvie drawers and jumped overboard with the stern line. To his surprise, the water was warm. Now that he noticed it, the weather this morning was definitely not what it had been for the last couple of weeks. He swam ashore but for once there could barely pull himself up the steep bank.

Gorson jumped in and helped him. They struggled a hundred yards to a gentler slope at the bottom of the minuscule canyon, then heaved until the *Alice* came drifting after them. Eventually her stern was made fast to one of the tiny oaks.

'If there's a spring it'll be up there,' Gorson said. They hadn't gone more than a hundred feet through the scrub oaks before Joe wished he'd had his shoes thrown ashore.

But the ridge couldn't be more than a quarter mile. To hell with it, he decided; if Gorson could make it barefoot he could. The wind flapped his wet skivvies over his thighs and gave him a slight chill. Within another hundred yards he was sweating.

The canyon was narrow and steep but unfortunately for their bare feet it was covered with soil instead of rock. Close-cropped grass grew under the umbrella-like covering of oak whose lower leaves had been browsed clean by goats. 'Odd,' Joe muttered.

'What?' Gorson panted.

'We've had seagulls with us during the wildest weather, yet here's a perfect roosting place and not a single bird.'

They plodded upward until they found the spring. It was so small that its overflow did not form a visible stream but seeped downward through the canyon's small triangular cross-section of soil. It was a clear, semi-circular pool in the rocks, about the size of the *Alice's* galley sink, and with a clear, sandy bottom. Joe flopped down and lowered his face for a cautious sip. 'Tastes clean,' he said. 'With the island uninhabited, chances are it is.'

'Uninhabited?' Gorson repeated.

Joe looked up. Facing them across the tiny clearing stood a girl. She was tanned but of an obviously blonde race. She wore her hair in a braid which had been twisted into a high crown held in place with thorns. She wore a necklace and bracelets of some blue stone. She wore nothing else. Joe stared awestruck, waiting for her to shriek or run. She watched them with an expectant, hopeful expression.

Joe glanced down. 'Caught in my drawers again,' he muttered.

'What?' Gorson asked.

'Nothing,' Joe said.

The girl beckoned. When they still stared she apparently tired of standing. She lay down in the short cropped grass and waited.

Gorson exploded into laughter. 'What a place for a whorehouse!' he roared. 'I wonder how business it?'

Something, Joe kept telling himself, is wrong. In the first place, there shouldn't be any island here. And now this! He wasn't dreaming. He was sweating and out of breath and his feet hurt. Gorson couldn't possibly laugh that loud in a dream. They went around the spring to where the girl still reclined in the grass.

'Do you speak English?' Joe asked.

A pleading smile.

'Ask if she's got a private room somewhere,' Gorson said.

Joe tried again in Raquel's Tenth Century Spanish but the girl only smiled. 'Oh hell!' he said, 'this isn't really happening.' He turned around to reassure himself—and faced two more naked girls.

'Holy Neptune,' Joe muttered.

The girl recognised a god's name: '*Roumánu*'? she asked.

Roumánu—Roman!

'No,' Joe said. '*Non sum Románus.*'

'Ah.' There was polite disappointment in the girl's tone. 'Are you?'

'*Roumánu*' *egó*?' She gave a fluting laugh and slipped into some form of bastard Greek which Joe could follow only vaguely. He sighed and tried to keep his eyes on her face. Damn women! Maybe he'd stumbled into a Tenth Century nudist colony. When in Rome . . . His eyes strayed back to those firm, upward pointing . . .

'Where are we?' he asked. 'What is this island?'

It sounded like Phryxos and rang no bell with Joe.

'What's she saying?' Gorson asked.

'I'm trying to find out where we are. Where's Spain? Hispania—Iberia. Lusitania?'

She shrugged and those pink tipped things jiggled.

'Where's Africa?'

Understanding glinted in the blonde's eyes. She pointed. Joe stared and did a double take. Unless the sun was crazy, this blonde was pointing due south.

'Where's Rome?' he persisted. She pointed vaguely west. 'Impossible,' Joe said. 'We're in the Atlantic.' But a horrible suspicion was growing on him. That warm water— this balmy climate. And what was a volcanic island doing in this part of the Atlantic? *'Quô modô appallatur hoc mare?'* he asked—how is this sea named?

'Agaios.'

'Aegean!' Joe shook his head. Even without a sextant he couldn't be that far off. But another thought struck him. 'What year is this?'

The girl stared.

'Are you Christian?'

No reaction.

'Moslem?' Still no reaction.

Joe knew damned well he'd been in the Atlantic last night. The last jump in space had also been a jump in time. Was this one? How was a history professor to know when people wouldn't keep track of time? 'Who is your god?' he asked.

The first girl had given up wriggling in the grass and came around the pool to join the other two. 'Aphrodite,' she said.

'Venus,' the other girl corrected. 'He speaks Latin.'

'It figures,' Joe muttered. He passed a hand over his eyes and tried again. 'What,' he asked, 'is Caesar's name?'

'Gaius Octavius.'

Joe felt a thrill of recognition. That tied it down to, let's see . . . He took over in 31 B.C. and died in 14 A.D. But there were too damn many Gaii in Roman history. 'Is this Gaius the adopted son of Julius Caesar?' The girls nodded.

'What're they saying?' Gorson asked.

'Later,' Joe said. By one felicitous stroke he had located them within forty-five years—but this, as he recalled, was a turbulent time, even though the Romans preferred to regard it as the Augustan Peace. Another thought came.

'Augustus?' he asked.

The girls looked blank.

'Is Gaius Octavius called Augustus?'

The girls were unsure.

'Is he young?'

They nodded.

And that tied it down: Gaius Octavius took over in 31 B.C. In 27 he assumed the title Augustus. Joe decided to quit while he was ahead.

'Is this a nudist colony?' Gorson asked. 'Why aren't they wearing clothes?'

'Forget to ask,' Joe parenthesised. 'How many of you are there on this island?'

The girls preferred not to understand. 'How many *you*?' one finally countered.

Joe decided it was his turn to avoid an answer.

Gorson was frantic. 'What're they saying?' he insisted.

'Getting information's like pulling teeth,' Joe explained, 'but I think . . .' He was about to say they'd gone back another thousand years, then—he didn't quite know why— he decided not to.

'How many you?' the girl was insisting.

'Many,' Joe said. 'Brave men, well armed. Where is your camp? Are you natives?' He was only talking to two girls now. He wondered when and where the others had disappeared. 'We were on our way to Rome,' one girl explained.

'Where from?'

The name was meaningless to Joe. 'Were you going to Rome or being taken there?' Again the girls opted not to understand. 'Do you want to go Rome or back home?'

'Rome!' they clamoured. 'Rome, Rome! No home, Rome!'

'What's all this about Rome?' Gorson asked.

'The girls want to go.'

'What was all that pointing awhile ago?'

'Trying to get my bearings,' Joe said hastily. 'We'd better get back down before they start worrying.'

'But why no clothes?'

'A good question,' Joe decided. He asked.

The girls gave him an odd look. 'Hot,' one finally said. 'Same as you.' Again Joe was reminded that he and Gorson wore only gape-fronted skivvy drawers.

'Well,' he said awkwardly, 'we'll see you later. Got to get back to the ship, you know.'

'Stay,' the girls insisted. One grabbed Joe's arm and rubbed against him.

'Really,' Joe said, 'We must be going. We can, uh talk about it later.' He turned around. '*Gorson!* On your feet now, let's go!' He caught the chief's arm and dragged him off downhill.

There was a noise below them, a murmur of male voices, a tramping of feet. Joe felt a sudden shrivelling. Their only path back to the *Alice* was cut off.

Girls hove into sight again, skipping gaily up the path with the agility of the island's goats. Behind them scrambled the entire crew of the *Alice*.

Joe stared aghast. They were all there—Cook, Guilbeau, Freedy, Rose . . . The Moorish prisoners scrambled along with the rest, all with eyes only for the naked blondes. Even Dr. Krom and the *imam* panted along in the rear of the pack, a highly unpaternal gleam in his ancient eyes.

'Whaddaya think of that?' Gorson marvelled.

Joe didn't know what to think. The girl was pulling on his arm, rubbing against him again. 'Do you have anything to eat?' he finally asked.

The girl had been in business long enough to realise that some hungers were stronger than others. 'Goat,' she said. 'Snared one last night.'

The men of the *Alice* came momentarily to their senses at the sight of Joe and Gorson.

'Ain't you ever seen a woman before?' Gorson growled.

'Not for several weeks,' Guilbeau answered.

'How many girls are there on this island?' Joe insisted.

'Enough to go around,' one of them answered.

'Any men?'

'Been some time since the men've had liberty sir,' Gorson suggested.

'There'll be time enough for that later. We've got to get water aboard and try to catch some of these goats. Here, now, all hands come back here!'

Guilbeau had caught a blonde and they collapsed in a giggling heap behind a rock. Several new girls had appeared, all wearing only anklets and bracelets. One, Jo noted, was not blonde. She was dark and looked like a slightly more voluptuous version of Raquel. She was squirting wine from a goatskin into Dr. Krom's mouth.

And where was Raquel? She must have stayed alone aboard the *Alice*. He looked for Gorson but the chief had disappeared. So had the blonde who clung to him.

'All hands now, come on and stop this foolishness. We've got to get to work!' The clearing was empty. Joe walked away from the spring and stumbled into a hollow between two oaks. 'Beat it!' Schwartz snapped. 'Go and find your own girl.'

Joe wandered incredulously around the clearing. He'd lost complete control. Neptune curse all women! No wonder no captain in his right mind would have them aboard ship.

Joe's historian half had been probing for several minutes. What was the name of the island where Circe turned Ulysses' men into pigs?

Rounding another boulder, he came across the aged *imam*. A redhead with a half-sprouted figure was feeding him

93

grapes. The grapes were very small and the corners of the *imam*'s beard dropped dark purple stains.

So what's wrong with me? Joe wondered. *After all, it is a good liberty port.* He looked around but there were no unattached girls in sight. Oh well, he sour graped, at least he wouldn't be on sick list nine days from now. He wondered what Raquel was doing back on the *Alice*. He ought to go back down and see if she was all right. But why go alone? In a hour or two he could pry the men loose and they could come back with a load of wood or water or something.

For the time being no one was going to listen to him. He would only make things worse by flapping around like a mother hen. Might as well climb to the top of the ridge and get a look around. If they really were in the Aegean there might be another island in sight.

He climbed slowly to the top of the ridge, acutely conscious by now that he should have gone back for his shoes. There was neither soil nor tree above the spring but the black volcanic rock had weathered so that the broken-bubble edges of its numerous small caves did not cut his feet.

After fifteen minutes of leisurely climb he topped the ridge and sat. The tiny horseshoe harbour and a miniature *Alice* were laid out below him like a scale drawing. While he watched, a faint gust rippled the harbour's narrow surface, the ripples breaking as they crossed the long painter stretching from the yawl's bow to the pinnacle. The Mediterranean, as he recalled, was not much for tides. That was one less worry. He looked about the cloudless horizon. A faint smudge to the nothwest might be land but he wasn't sure.

Going down was harder than climbing up. His stubbed toes were bleeding by the time he reached the spring.

The fine edge of the *Alice*'s collective appetite was dulled by now. They had emerged from their several nooks for a more leisurely debauch. The goat revolved over a small fire. The *Alice's* men, paired off with the blondes and a single brunette, were guzzling wine.

Gorson reared up on one elbow to stare blearily at him. 'Shay, Mr. Rate,' he asked, 'what year we in?'

There was sudden silence as every eye fixed on Joe.

Damn you, Gorson. Ishtar shrivel your gonadia! He had planned to break the news gently. Or had he intended to tell them at all? They stared, suspicious now and distrusting. He sighed and took the bull by the horns. 'Last night,' he said, 'remember that bump when we stayed underwater so long and all at once Freedy got a different fathometer reading? It must've been working all right after all.' A bell was beginning to ring somewhere in Joe's head but he ignored it. 'This time we came out at low tide or something. Anyhow, we weren't at sea level.'

'What year is it?'

'I don't know. About 28 or 20 B.C.'

'*Before Christ?*'

Joe started to explain about Augustus.

Gorson turned to the rest of the crew. 'Know what I think,' he said, 'I think he done it on purpose. He's a history nut. He wants to go on back instead of getting us home!'

The silence was more ominous now. Lapham, Dr. Krom's college boy assistant, looked uneasily at Joe. 'Is it true?' he asked.

'No,' Joe said distractedly, for he was suddenly aware that he knew how their time jumps were happening.

'When you gonna take us home?' Rose asked.

'How should I know?'

'You're supposed to know everything,' Gorson growled.

'I know one one thing,' Joe snapped. 'If you want to get home it'll be easier after you've forgotten these trollops and get some water in the *Alice's* tanks. And how about snaring a few dozen goats so we can dry the meat—providing the Roman coast guard doesn't patrol here too often.'

The blondes were restless with all this talk. They had the entertainer's instinct for crisis even if they didn't understand the language. One appeared from nowhere, bearing several fresh skins of wine.

'Three cheers for Mr. Rate,' Cookie yelled. 'It's been at least a month since I've had a liberty like this!'

Gorson swayed to his feet. 'You can't get away with this,' he growled. 'I've read the book. I know my rights.' From four feet away the brunette squirted an unerring red jet into Gorson's mouth. He choked on the wine and began coughing. While the others were still laughing Joe walked off.

What were these girls doing here in the first place? Where was all that wine coming from? It took a press and vats to make wine. This island was honeycombed with caves but he was sure none was big enough to hide that kind of installation.

Away from the noise of the party, he collapsed on the shady side of an oak and piled handfulls of damp leaf mould over his bleeding toes. He'd probably get hookworm or bilharzia but he was too disgusted to care. He dozed off and dreamt of a triumphal march through the streets of Rome. The triumph dissolved into a gladitorial display with Joe on the wrong end of the sword. He spoke abruptly and rolled off the rock which had been stabbing him.

The sun had gone down and the hours of inactivity without clothing or cover had left him thoroughly chilled. He clambered stiffly to his feet and limped back up to the spring. There was no sound now. The *Alice's* men sprawled in weird attitudes around the demolished goat. Joe shook one. He grunted but did not waken. Worriedly, Joe made the rounds. All were breathing but he didn't believe they could be so uniformly drunk. Thank Neptune he hadn't tasted the wine.

There was not a girl in sight.

With a sinking in his stomach, Joe realised what was up.

Should have stayed awake, he told himself. Should have gone down to the *Alice*. But he hadn't. Come to think of it, what could he have done alone? He threw branches on the embers where the goat had barbecued and when that blazed up he found the broken bottom of an amphora the girls had kept wine in. The spike bottomed jar fragment held about a gallon.

Straddling Gorson, he poured a gallon of spring water. The bos'n sputtered. By the third slosh he was on his feet and swearing.

'Yes, I did it,' Joe said. 'Now listen you turgid testicled slob—you bigmouthed yourself into this, now bigmouth yourself out. You're captain from now on.'

Gorson gazed blearily about the clearing and saw the *Alice's* men. Abruptly, he was wide awake and sober. 'Jesus, what do we do now?'

Joe savoured his moment of glory. 'One of the first things you can do is stand at attention when you address your captain.'

Gorson gulped. 'Yessir,' he said. 'I'm sorry sir, I . . .'

'Get these men on their feet and let's get back to the ship.'

Gorson grabbed the amphora bottom and started carrying water. Ten minutes later they stood in the firelight. Dr. Krom's bushy head fitted his sheepish look. 'All right,' Joe growled, 'you've hit your first foreign port on this cruise. You've been rolled and you've probably all got a dose. Are you ready to go back aboard?' He stopped and looked at them carefully. Raquel, he knew, was aboard the *Alice*. Someone else was missing. 'Where's McGrath?'

'His Holiness stayed aboard,' Villegas said.

The cold knifed deeper into Joe's stomach. McGrath had been increasingly unstable since that clout on the head. Was Raquel safe? At least the little god shouter hadn't stampeded ashore after those blonde trollops. He remembered the tooth marks and Raquel's cryptic comment. They'd been alone all day. But what the hell, he thought, she can take care of herself. If she wants to.

The *Alice*'s men still stood in a numbed group, awakening to their position. They had carried no weapons to begin with. Now their pockets were empty. Joe put them to gathering rocks. When each had filled his pockets and bagged a few inside his shirt they lit firebrands. The oak would not blaze long but with luck it would light them partway down the hill.

Joe's feet were so sore by now that he could hardly walk. *Ought to make Gorson carry me.* But he didn't. They started down the valley. Joe tried to remember if there'd been a moon last night. It was very dark now under the oaks and they had not progressed a hundred yards before a torch went out. Halfway down the slope the last brand was extinguished. They fumbled along, bumping into trees, stumbling over roots.

There was a splash as Red Schwartz abruptly found himself neck-deep in the bay. He splashed a great deal and took the Lord's name in vain before he caught an outstretched hand and pulled himself back ashore. They fanned out, searching for the *Alice*'s mooring line. They didn't find it.

'Gotta be here,' Gorson was grumbling. There was a worried tone in his voice. 'Whole canyon's not a hundred yards wide. How could we miss it?'

Joe glanced back uphill at the faint glow where they'd left the fire. It was not the fire he was seeing. The moon was about to rise from behind the ridge. It did and there was no sign of the *Alice*.

Weaponless, miserable, hungover, they looked hopefully at Joe. 'Does anyone think this is my fault?' he needled.

The *imam* and his Moors huddled to one side, looking ever more disconsolate. Joe decided not to rub it in. The moon rose higher until its direct rays illuminated the pinnacle in the small harbour's centre. And there they saw the *Alice*. Someone had cut the stern line and taken up on the bow line. It was a good hundred yards to the yawl's stern. Joe turned to the *imam*. 'Ask your men if they can swim,' he said.

'Why ask?'

Dr. Krom would probably have a heart attack if he tried. 'How about the rest of you?' The navy men nodded. 'Can you do it with rocks in your pockets and come up fighting?' This time they weren't so sure.

Joe put them to gathering logs. There was neither time nor tools to make a raft but they could swim the trunks out, using them to rest on. He tried to imagine what they would face aboard the *Alice*. The girls would all be there, of course. Soft and alluring as they might seem, Joe suspected they would be a match for exhausted hungover men trying to pull themselves aboard the *Alice*. And what if they had a few men of their own along?

Again he wondered how they'd happened to land on this island. If the girls had been going to Rome they must've been shipwrecked or marooned. If shipwrecked, what sort of miracle drowned the whole crew while they saved not only themselves but apparently hundreds of gallons of wine?

Retaking the *Alice* was not going to be easy. But . . . whoever boarded her had to sail her away. Engines would be an impenetrable mystery. Perhaps the halliard winches were also beyond them. Had they already discovered they couldn't sail her? Probably just waiting for a wind. He was composing a silent prayer for continued calm when the first ripple of breeze hit them from behind. The *Alice* could cut loose and drift out of the harbour mouth now.

'Will you get on the ball with those logs?' he snapped. A rumble and splash answered him as they finally man-handled one into the water. 'All hands in and see if it'll support us.'

It could, so they began swimming. 'Not crossways, for Christ's sake!' Joe growled. 'Turn it lengthways.' Strung along both sides, they paddled with one hand and kicked their slow way toward the *Alice*.

What had happened to Raquel and McGrath by now? Something else bothered him too. It kept bothering him during the twenty minutes it took to paddle out. Finally, as the log bumped gently into the *Alice's* stern, he re-remembered the name of the island where Circe had turned Ulysses' men into pigs. It was Aeaea.

7

The log bumped again and Joe mentally cursed. No one seemed to be standing watch. Gorson and Cookie had already pulled half the crew on deck. The log bumped a third time and Joe forced himself between it and the stern. The breeze kept pushing it toward them but he couldn't cast it adrift until everyone was aboard. He wondered why the *Alice* stood stern to the breeze until he came aboard and saw that she had drifted round and round until the bow line was hopelessly snarled. The pinnacle was grinding paint away from the bow. 'Women!' he muttered.

The deck was deserted. Gorson went forward with half the men while Joe led the remainder to the after scuttle. With rocks at the ready they oozed down both hatchways and converged on the galley.

The forecastle was dark. The only light aboard glowed dimly in the curtained galley. Joe stood in the after hatchway and saw Gorson staring aghast from the forecastle. Between them the galley was stuffed with girls. Not nude— naked was the only word.

Facing a bulkhead, Howard McGrath cringed in one corner. He had both his arms firmly over his face. Raquel, still wearing a dress, sat with the other girls, listening intently to an enormously fat woman dressed in the remains of a flowing, Grecian style garment. She squatted crosslegged on the settee and spoke in an unknown language.

When she glanced up and saw Joe her bulging cheeks rearranged themselves into a smile which exposed several gold teeth. 'Tell me, sonny, she said, 'did Al Smith win or are we still stuck with Prohibition?'

I'm going nuts, Joe thought dazedly. But he realised he was cutting no ice with the crew by standing there looking stupid.

'Cat got your tongue, sonny?' the fat woman asked. 'From the looks of the still I'd say we're still in prohibition.' A tremendous sigh rippled up and down her abdomen. 'It's been a hell of a while since I had a drink of good stuff.'

'Wha—What year are we in?' Joe finally managed.

'Couldn't say, sonny. When I first hit town I looked for a Salvation Army soup kitchen. Near's I make it, there ain't a Christer in town.'

Gorson elbowed through the mass of naked femininity. 'Where you from?' he asked the fat woman.

'Windy City,' she wheezed. 'You can call me Ma Trimble. Sorry about making you swim, sonny—I wasn't expecting the navy.'

'Why didn't you come back for us?'

'We were going to if we ever got untangled from this danged rock. Hell, sonny, I never could drive a flivver, much less a boat.'

McGrath squirmed in his corner. Still hunched with arms over eyes, he turned. 'Mr. Rate,' he asked, 'is that you?'

'Sorry about him,' Ma Trimble said. 'One of my girls chunked a rock at him when he came aboard. When he came to . . .'

McGrath peeped out cautiously. He immediately ducked his head between his knees again 'I thought I'd gone to hell,' he said muffledly.

Red Schwartz stepped over a couple of blondes and lifted the befuddled puritan to his feet, half carrying him into the forecastle.

Joe surveyed the packed galley helplessly. 'What did you intend to do with my ship?' he asked.

Ma Trimble shrugged. 'Anything beats starving to death on a rockpile. How was I to guess you were Americans?'

'But how are we all—don't you have beds or anything ashore? And damn it, Mrs. Trimble, you're going to have to get some clothes on these girls.'

'Look who's talking,' the old woman laughed.

Joe glanced down at his shorts. 'We can't all sleep here,' he said. 'How did you happen to land on this island, any-how?'

Ma Trimble waved a pudgy hand. 'That, sonny,' she warned, 'is a long story.'

It was indeed, and Ma Trimble told it complete with ex-pansive gestures and colourful expressions that set Mc-Grath to trembling anew. What it all boiled down to was that Ma Trimble had grown a bit desperate when three of the best customers at her establishment had gone blind from the booze she served. The booze was sold to her in accord-ance with what the mob politely called an 'exclusive con-tract,' and Ma had no desire to cause the boys to lose their politeness—but if only there was some way to make the stuff drinkable!

A friend came to the rescue. He knew, he said, a guy who'd 'studied chemistry down at Joliet,' and this un-worthy gentleman thought he could rig up a rectifying still to salvage the stuff. Ma Trimble grasped at the straw, the still was constructed on a houseboat out on Goose Island, and . . .

WHAM!

She awoke alone, afloat on an endless blue sea. Lake Michigan's sky could not possibly be this blue. Besides, Ma suspected Lake Michigan was not salty.

Four days passed before a trader from Britain took her

off the sagging houseboat. Despairing of ever realising a plugged denarius from this fat old savage, he deposited her bedraggled and friendless on Tyre's waterfront.

Ma Trimble was the type who would land on her feet anywhere, and that included ancient Tyre. Even so, there were several terrible months while she learned the language, the angles, and the local law's blind spots. It was nearly a year before she acquired a tiny crib and stocked it with a sloe-eyed, shopworn Syrian bint of some fourteen winters. She taught the girl a couple of Midwest tricks which hadn't as yet caught on in the Middle East, and the establishment flourished, adding four more girls in the course of time.

One of her most frequent customers was one Publius Suilius Libellus, the Roman Colonel of this gook garrison town. He was, in fact, such a good customer that when Ma Trimble pointed out the many advantages he could gain by taking Ma and her girls to the Big City—as opposed to the disadvantages of Ma's confiding all she knew to Publius' wife, the daughter of his commanding officer—Publius then and there decided he'd always wanted to get back to Rome.

The *Astarte* was still in sight of Tyre's chalk cliffs when it began blowing, and there wasn't much the crew could do about their course, which was now in the general direction of Athens. By the fourth day out, though, a cone-shaped island thrust itself inexorably out of the sea before them. A wreck was obviously unavoidable, so Publius, a Roman soldier to the end, had himself and his wife lowered in a boat along with the crew, abandoning Ma and her girls along with the doomed *Astarte* as he made for shore.

It was a small boat which went under, however, swamped by a huge wave. Four of Ma's girls continued pumping water from the *Astarte's* bilges with the ship's bucket and chain apparatus, while one of them promised a white rooster to Hecate. Without pressure on her helm the ship wallowed straight for vertical cliffs. The girl upped her offer to two roosters. When the cliffs were a hundred paces away she made her final firm bid of five roosters.

The ship slipped easily into a small, horseshoe-shaped harbour.

They got some wine ashore and removed their supplies up to the spring. Next day they'd return to the half-sunk hulk and dive for their clothes. That night the storm front collapsed and sea level raised two inches. The hulk floated gently away.

Joe stretched and looked around the *Alice's* crowded galley. McGrath had returned to the galley doorway and permitted his eyes to rest for longer intervals on the naked blondes, an odd, almost calculating expression on his face.

Now that he had his ship back, Joe wondered what he was going to do with the women. 'We'll, maybe we can give you a lift someplace where you can catch a boat for Rome,' he said hopefully.

Ma Trimble gave a short, hard laugh. 'Not on your tin-type, sonny. It would've been rough enough with protection. You won't catch me going there without old Publius.'

'But what can I do?'

'You're navy, sonny. You can take a distressed American citizen home where she belongs.'

'But what about these . . .' He groped for a word to describe the girls.

'It'll look awful funny if you leave 'em behind,' Ma Trimble said. 'Mr. Hoover'd call 'em refugees.'

Joe looked helplessly around the *Alice*. Freedy and Rose focused their attention on the ceiling. McGrath studied Joe with an odd, eager look. Guilbeau and Villegas were silently communicating with a couple of girls. So was Schwartz. Dr. Krom and his civilian assistant studied the cabin sole. Cook glanced at Joe and shrugged. Gorson added his own shrug. 'I think we're stuck, sir,' he said.

The *imam* and his boys understood nothing so Joe ignored them. Raquel had picked up some English; he wasn't sure how much. Remembering all the dresses she'd taken from the Viking women, he said, 'How about getting these girls covered up?'

Raquel nodded and visibly thawed toward him.

'All right,' Joe said. 'Gorson, take a couple of men and get that bow line untangled.' The moon was high, so they had little trouble warping the *Alice* back ashore. Joe posted watches and went to bed.

Dawn brought a strange boat to the harbour mouth. Joe studied it through binoculars. Nobody aboard. The antique was typically Greek, with high bow and a fiddle pegged stern post like a gondola. Joe wondered how far the eighteen footer had drifted from its fishing village. And why couldn't it have turned up last night when he'd needed a skiff?

He turned the *Alice* inside out and found no chlorine tablets. The spring water was sweet but the rocks were lined with moss. In three weeks' time the *Alice* would draw green streamers from her faucets. There was neither time nor dry wood to boil it all.

McGrath edged up, still wearing that odd, eager look. 'Mr. Rate,' he asked, 'why can't we stay here?'

'Too close to Roman shipping lanes,' Joe answered. 'The coast guard's liable to drop in on us any day.'

The little god shouter nodded and walked silently away.

Joe put the girls and all hands to relaying water downhill in such buckets and amphorae as were available.

'How about wine?' Ma Trimble asked.

Joe was not entranced with its vinegary, turpentined taste but it might keep the water from turning. Mixed with water it would also be less likely to make the crew turn. 'Pour it in the tanks,' he said, and inspected Ma Trimble's cheese. It was white and hard, could be crumbled only with

106

a mallet. Joe hoped it didn't carry dysentery. The wheat flour she'd saved would help relieve their diet.

Rose produced a hammer and saw. He and Gorson began rigging bunks in every corner.

Goats overran the island, but one bullet was worth more than one goat. Joe wondered if they had an archer aboard and learned the Moors were all swordsmen. Slinging, he learned after a few wild throws, was hopeless—and the goats were too smart to walk into a pitfall.

He was unenthusiastically considering a catapult zeroed in on the trail when Dr. Krom edged up apologetically. 'They drink water, don't they?' the old man asked.

Joe cursed himself and began fencing the spring. Three days later they had no difficulty running down goats. Cookie and Lapham rigged drying racks and organised Ma Trimble's girls to keep seagulls from stealing the meat. None appeared. Joe was mildly surprised. Birds were abnormally sensitive to air pollution. He wondered if the extinct volcano was still giving off a trace of gas which scared them away. The water was chilly and the weather noticeably rawer on the open side of the island. He asked Dr. Krom about it and the old man thoughtfully inverted test tubes in the water around the *Alice*.

Next day the water in the tubes had been partially displaced by something. The old man sniffed one and spent several hours fussing over the others with his small cabinet of reagents.

A week passed and they had flour, rye, and dried meat. The mid-harbour pinnacle's rope-worn grooves left Joe scant hope that they could remain long unvisited here. Shortly after supper Red Schwartz edged up to him. 'Mr. Rate,' he asked, 'you seen Howie today?'

'Why no, wasn't he off with the woodcutters?'

'He didn't come ashore this morning. I thought you'd kept him aboard on some other detail.'

'He'll turn up.'

Dr. Krom ambled up in his stiff, old man's gait and proffered a bottle. Joe sniffed and wrinkled his nose at the remainder of froth chemistry and hydrogen sulphide. 'Out of the water in this crater?' he asked.

Krom nodded. 'Nearly a cubic centimeter in only forty-eight hours.'

At least Joe now knew why there hadn't been any sea-gulls. He caught Raquel's arm as as she hurried by and asked her to put some girls to mending the *Alice's* tattered sails.

To Ma Trimble life was basically a freeload. Raquel had taken over the girls and even gotten the mountain-fleshed madam to do a little work on occasion. Joe found himself depending more and more on her and noted that she stank less often. Come to think of it, since the blondes had come aboard she had been positively radiant. What gave?

That night they brought a half-dozen goats aboard and tore down the fence around the spring. With any luck the fresh meat would last to Gibraltar. Joe climbed the volcano's peak and studied the sky. Wind blew briskly outside the harbour. He debated getting underway this evening, then remembered the girls would still be sewing on the mains'l. Abruptly, he remembered Schwartz's god shouting friend. What was with McGrath?

The sun had set an hour ago but he could still see the island clearly save for a tiny stretch just outside one of the horseshoe wings which enclosed the harbour. He wondered what McGrath was doing alone. Tired of all the fornication aboard the *Alice*? Joe felt a fleeting sympathy and wondered why he too desisted. The girls were attractive and eager. So far no one had reported sick. To whom was he being faithful?

He took a final look around. There was no sign of life on the island. Schwartz and Gorson were waiting worriedly when he reached the *Alice*. 'Isn't he back yet?' Joe asked.

McGrath was still lost. *Should have talked to him,* Joe

thought. The boy had had that odd, half awakened look since Ma Trimble's naked legion had piled aboard. Maybe they'd whacked him too hard and some of the Outer Darkness was seeping in through a crack in his skull.

'It's been over twenty-four hours,' Schwartz said, 'Maybe he drowned or fell into one of those caves.'

Joe sighed. He wondered if he'd been too anxious to study the past. Could he have gotten them out of here a day or two earlier?

'. . . a search,' Gorson was suggesting.

'Right. Make up some torches. I'll see if there's a glimmer left in the flashlight.' It was dark. The galley would have seemed deserted had it not been for the snickers, giggles and rustlings which came from all corners. Something seemed to be wrong with the latch on Joe's cubicle. He twisted again and the knob suddenly opened.

The flashlight wasn't in the shallow drawer under the chart table. Must be in his bunk. He fumbled and felt legs in darkness. 'Now who the hell?' After an eternity he found the light switch. He blinked several times before recognising Howie McGrath. Then he noticed what the little god shouter held in his hand. Joe looked straight into the muzzle of his own pistol.

8

Howard McGrath had been born illegitimate—Sadie's Sin, as his guilt-holy mother had kept calling him.

Don't look at girls or you'll burn in hell, she had said.

Don't touch whiskey; it's the Devil's Drink.

Don't say naughty words or God won't love you.

Mother won't love you.

Don't touch.

Don't drink.

Don't say.

Don't think.

DON'T!

That confused business of the woman, the snake and the apple: somehow it all led to little Howie, born evil, who must fight constantly lest the evil within him break out and carry him to everlasting hellfire.

His mother had not cried when he left home. The navy was the heaven of Satan's darlings and Howie was predestined.

The first few weeks in boot camp had been undiluted horror but Howie knew a greater horror was yet to come: evil companions would lead him into sin and the degradation. They would force him to drink whiskey!

He had been surprised and vaguely disappointed when no one invited him to debauchery. All told, his first liberty turned out to be as dull as the rest of Howie's short, hypersheltered life.

Came sea duty, the *Alice*. Red Schwartz was not on the

side of the angels. Red was going to fry in hellfire forever but he didn't seem to care. Whiskey-drinking, fornicating, hell-raising Red had survived five and a half years in the navy. Chances were he would last twenty-four and half more. Schwartz taught him all the things he hadn't learned in bootcamp and privately vowed he would someday squire this shivering young wretch through a brothel. But the time was still not ripe.

McGrath remained as virgin as a national forest. Some day *he* was going to see Red Schwartz washed in the Blood of the Lamb. But not just yet. If Schwartz were saved, Howie would be deprived of his only sinful pleasure—shuddering over Schwartz's embellished accounts of San Diego's Babylonian quarter.

While he remained aboard the *Alice* and the women remained in San Diego it had been easy to avoid sin. But with warm lithe women, all aquiver with sinful bulges, bumping into him in narrow passageways, sleeping practically within reach . . .

Satan had buried him under an avalanche of naked women!

Yet as he listened to Ma Trimble's long, rambling story it gradually occurred to Howie that these girls were from the Holy Land. That language must be the language Jesus spoke! Maybe they had seen Him. No, the time was a few years before Christ's birth. No point in going to Israel . . . but perhaps something greater offered itself. If he were to go to Rome, now . . . how much trouble would it be to locate young Pontius Pilate? Once he found him, and with Mr. Rate's pistol . . .

It was going to require co-operation from these girls. They seemed to have no English among them. Howie's opportunity came when all hands were lugging water down from the spring. She was small and dark, unlike the others. Though long past her apprenticeship, some accident of nature had given her a line of lip and jaw which suggested that the world was a very large and somewhat too complicated place for her. Had Howie stopped to analyse it, he would have realised she resembled nothing so much as a darker and less god-bound version of his mother. They stumbled down the trail together, each bearing an amphora of water. Pointing to himself, he said, 'Me Howard.'

She stared.

'Howard—my name's Howard.'

It came out 'yugger' when she said it. Pointing at her, he made a questioning mumble. Had he possessed a more detailed knowledge of Semitic vowel shifts Howie might have felt a premonitory shudder at her name. To him it sounded like Leilat'.

Lillith put down her water jar and squatted to rest. These *nautae* had been more insatiable than a mob of Roman dogfaces just in from desert patrol. And after putting in a full night's work this water detail was giving her aches in places she scarcely remembered. She had been about to tell this *nauta* to go bugger Pluto, but . . . Oh well, these young skinny ones hadn't the staying power of a starving rabbit. She lugged her amphora around behind a tree where it wouldn't be seen from the trail. Howie followed.

It was hot and she'd been running around this island naked for the last three weeks. Today she wore one of Raquel's high collared, long sleeved dresses—just the thing for an Iceland winter. She untied her waist cord and turned round so Howie could unbutton her. After a moment she turned again to see what was keeping him.

The idiot had some kind of miniature parchment book in his hand and a stylus in the other. Lillith was annoyed. Slowly it dawned on her that he hadn't turned her down; he hadn't even understood her offer. What did he want?

She undid the top two buttons at the back of her neck and fanned a little air into the bodice. Then she turned to Howie. 'Anáchnu Yuggerti?'

'Yes,' Howie said, 'I'm Howard. Anaknoo Leilat'?'

Soon he knew the words for eye, nose, mouth, arm, hand. Lillith fanned her bodice again and taught him the word for button. She ballooned out the heavy wool and blew into it. This damned tent was suffocating her! She fanned the skirt up and down.

He learned words for toe, foot, and ankle. Breathing rapidly, he progressed to knee. Howie had not realised learning a language could be so interesting. It was getting ungodly hot in this little hole between the oak's roots. He began to sympathise with Leilat' in that heavy woollen thing. She taught him the word for dress. Pointing at his belt, she said the word for buckle.

Howie was sure he'd never remember the words but she gave him no time to stop and review. Leilat' caught his hand and drew him towards her. She had another lesson in mind for him—and since it was Howie's first, it went very quickly.

In spite of Ma Trimble's change in plans, Lillith had no interest at all in visiting some outlandish country no one had ever heard of. She wanted to go to Rome. Obviously so did this timid young soul. Therefore . . .

Lessons progressed. Howie became obsessed with the magnificence of his plan: they would take the *Alice* to Rome and after he'd settled P. Pilate's hash there would be time to swing around by the Holy Land and give John the Baptist a briefing on his mission in life. Mr. Rate had been a history professor. He would be handy for taking care of details. Mr. Rate would go along with the plan, and the *Alice's* men would do whatever Mr. Rate told them. Mr. Rate wouldn't balk at a chance for Salvation. But some obscure instinct made Howie decide perhaps he'd better get hold of the gun first.

Joe felt neither shock nor amazement as Howie unfolded his magnificent project, only a bored sense of corroboration. It was so magnificently logical. His only wonder was how in hell he was going to get the pistol away from this addled god shouter.

'It's a big decision,' he finally said. 'When it comes to salvation each man should choose for himself. You wouldn't want me responsible for sending a man's soul to hell, would you?'

Howie shook his head.

'Well, let's call them in one at a time and tell them your plan. Those that don't want to go can stay on the island.'

Howie thought a moment. It sounded fair.

With his eye on the revolver which wobbled in Howie's sweaty hand, Joe opened the door a crack and called Gorson. The chief crowded into the tiny compartment. 'What the hell . . . ?' Abruptly he shut up, wondering if Joe's kick had shattered his ankle.

'Go ahead Howie; I'm sure the chief's interested.'

Howie told his story more smoothly this time, dwelling long on the glories of Salvation. Gorson listened noncommittally. When Howie was through and his blazing eyes awaited a decision for God or Satan the chief glanced at Joe for a hint. 'Well,' Joe said rapidly, 'it looks like you have the two of us with you. Who should we call next?'

'Cook, by all means,' the chief said.

The pistol had not left McGrath's hand. They were already jammed in like boots in a chow line. He opened the door a crack and called.

Cookie tried but there wasn't room in the tiny compartment. He had seen the pistol so Howie could not let him retreat. They faced each other for a tense moment.

'Tell you what,' Joe said. 'Howie, why don't you put the pistol in your pocket and follow us up on deck where we can get a breath of air?'

Howie was uncomfortable by now. He appreciated Mr. Rate's thoughtfulness. Up on deck they could reach some agreement. He had to be on his way soon. Suddenly he remembered . . . 'Just to show God you're on his side, we'll smash the still on the way up.'

Gorson gasped.

'Don't you want to?'

The bos'n looked imploringly at Joe. 'It's not the booze, Howie,' he finally said. Then he remembered the god shouter had no particular interest in returning to the Twentieth Century. He opened his mouth a couple of times but nothing came out.

'Ain't another piece of copper tubing like that in the whole world,' Cookie protested.

'We can talk it over later,' Joe suggested. Sooner or later this madman would fall asleep. How much damage would he do beforehand? In the back of Joe's mind lurked the uncomfortable thought that they might have to kill Howie. 'Why do you want to destroy the still?' he temporised.

Howie was shocked. 'Why Mr. Tate, you know it's against regulations. Whiskey is the Devil's Drink!'

'Well yes,' Joe hedged, 'but that still's made out of government property. You know, I'd be so busy filling out forms and writing reports, I don't know how I'd ever find time to help you with this Roman business.'

'Sure, kid,' Gorson contributed, 'you know how it is with those reports and paperwork. Why, old Commander Cutlott would have a haemorrhage.'

Howie was not buying it. His eyes twitched from Gorson to Cookie to Joe. Joe wondered why he had never before noticed how much white they showed. 'No,' Howie said firmly. 'The still has got to go.'

'But can't we . . . ?'

'Now!'

Joe opened the door and slowly stepped out. Dr. Krom crowded in front of him and waved test tubes. 'Later,' Joe said, and kept walking.

Dr. Krom wouldn't be brushed off. 'Urgent,' he was saying. 'Must act immediately.'

'What do you know about urgency?' Joe muttered. Another step and there was Krom again, clutching at his sleeve. The old man was in a real flap; his English had dwindled away into pure Hungarian.

'*Nyet, nyista*, whatever the hell it is in Magyar—no, damn it!' Joe said. '*Later*.'

There was a tinkling crash behind them. *There goes the still*. But all was not yet lost—they'd replaced one broken bell jar. But if that copper coil ever went over the side . . . Slowly, Joe turned.

The god shouter was backed up against the bulkhead, describing wild wavering arcs with a handful of pistol. 'Don't Howie,' Joe said. 'You're here to save souls, not send them to hell before they can choose.'

'I've got to get to Rome.'

'All right, all right. Has anyone said no? Look at all these poor souls seeking the light. Give them your message. I'll interpret.'

Howie frowned an instant, then began repeating his private evangel. After a moment Joe interrupted. '*Está loco*,' he said, '*Procuren no hacerle daño. Non compos mentis. Non respondit actâs suâs.*' He tried again in Greek, urging them not to kill the Salvation-addled Bible belter.

Howie had the heavenly reward bit down pat by now. Oh well, as long as he keeps talking, Joe philosphised. But that thrice accursed pistol still wobbled around, describing in great flamboyant arcs the riches of heaven. Howie raised both hands in a gesture of benediction and the pistol pointed momentarily upward. Joe caught movement from the corner of his eye—a whistling hiss as Raquel's knife removed the thinnest slice from Howie's already mangled ear. The pistol went off.

Ma Trimble screamed. Immediately the blondes made it in a capella choir. Howie stared at the pistol, wondering if he had caused all that noise. Something heavy struck him in the forehead. The *imam* hefted another cup. 'Takes one to catch one,' he said with a wolfish grin at Joe.

Fragments of heavy, handleless navy cup lay about the shattered saviour. His forehead bulged as if a third eye were ready to open. Raquel stepped over the crushed crusader and retrieved her knife. *That's the second time she's saved my life,* Joe thought.

Schwartz crowded up. 'Mr. Rate, what're we gonna do?'

'Can't let him run around loose. Get some merthiolate and cotton.'

Dr. Krom crowded up again, waving a test tube and spouting Magyar. 'Later,' Joe said, but the excitement had blown a fuse somewhere in the old man. 'Cookie, fix him up.'

Cookie nodded and returned a moment later with a half cup of cloudy liquid. Dr. Krom took the cup absently and drank it. He coughed and abruptly spoke English. 'Most urgent,' he began. Abruptly, his eyes crossed. He sat heavily on the settee.

'Foreigners just ain't got no stomach,' Cookie observed.

'Did we leave anything ashore?' Joe asked.

Gorson shook his head. 'What're you gonna do with him?' he asked, pointing at McGrath.

'How should I know?' Joe snapped. He knelt again. McGrath's pulse was steady and regular. He peeled back eyelids and both pupils were the same size. No blood from nose or ears. 'Lapham!' he yelled.

'Sir,' that young man asked, 'what did you give Dr. Krom?'

'A drink. Get the hammer, saw, and find some nails.'

'I'll try, sir.'

The young civilian had suddenly started stirring him. Why? He caught Cookie's eye and they bore the young god shouter forward. 'Any of your things in the chain locker?' he asked Raquel.

She shook her head.

They made McGrath as comfortable as possible atop the jumble of nylon line. Lapham reappeared with some odds and ends of lumber. 'Leave room between these slats so we can feed him,' Joe said.

Where was Gorson? Joe went on deck and found the chief fumbling in the darkness, trying to shackle the mains'l headboard into its halliard. 'Girls were sewing this afternoon,' he explained. 'It's unbent.'

It was nearly midnight. Working in the dark, they could take all night bending on the mains'l and then run the risk of tearing it. In daylight it would only take minutes. 'Get some sleep,' Joe said. 'We'll get underway at dawn.' The bos'n nodded and went below.

Joe took a deep breath and reached for a cigarette. When would he remember there weren't any? He needed a shave too but they'd been out of soap for three weeks and he kept putting off the thought of another scrape with that same old blade.

Were they ready for another try at the Azores? He wandered around the yawl's deck, testing the standing rigging with his hand. It was stainless so there was no rust problem, but the *Alice* had taken several hard knocks. Were there any incipient cracks in shackles or turnbuckles? He meandered up into the bows and ran a speculative hand over the forestay. Someone scooted aside to keep from being stepped on. He squinted and saw Raquel. 'Sorry about crowding you out of the chain locker,' he said.

'I have not slept there for some time.'

'Oh?' Too hot, he supposed.

'I do not enjoy what goes on in the forecastle.'

'Nor I,' Joe agreed. 'Perhaps they'll settle down when we get to sea.'

'Haven't we worked hard enough here?'

Joe sighed. He hadn't realised how weary he was. He sat and leaned against the anchor winch. Ought to go below, he knew, but all that rustling and giggling filtered into his cubicle. It was cooler up here and the moon was just setting beyond the harbour mouth. His head was resting on something soft but he was too tired to see what.

Somewhat later he heard people moving quietly along the deck again but again his exhaustion wouldn't let him care why anyone would be throwing things into the caïque he'd salvaged that morning.

He woke to the bleary realisation that Raquel had sat all night cradling his head in her lap. She felt him move and dumped him unceremoniously on deck. He scrambled to his feet and started yelling the *Alice's* crew awake. He stopped with an 'all hands' choked crossways as he saw what Raquel stared at. Less than twenty feet away a large bireme was moored. At least eighty oars were visible on Joe's side. Through the oar ports he caught glimpses of rowers. They looked mean.

He dived down the forward scuttle, dragging Raquel after him. 'Stay below,' he shouted. 'Let's get the hell out of here!' Hurling blondes like a berserk snowplough, he lifted the floorboard over the engine.

Rose spun valves. He opened fuel cocks, water cocks, and exhaust cocks. The starter began grinding. Nothing happened. Rose gave a disgusted grunt and reached for the ether bottle. He poured a capful into the air intake. The diesel gave a shuddering explosion and roared into life.

'Full ahead!' Joe yelled.

'We're tied up.'

'It's light line. Try to break it.'

The *Alice* trembled and moved a foot or two. Joe stationed himself at a porthole. 'Reverse!' he yelled. The *Alice* took up slack in the bow line which stretched to the midharbour pinnacle. 'Now full ahead!'

The yawl lunged forward again. She made all of six feet. Aboard the bireme Romans stared at this ship which roared and moved without oarsman. Joe wondered if fear of the supernatural would keep them from boarding. Then he remembered the fixed Roman policy of destroying everything they mistrusted or misunderstood.

Cook was edging around the open engine compartment. Joe took the cleaver from him. 'But Mr. Rate . . .' He saw Joe's face and abruptly stopped. Joe eased the hatch open. The line came through an eye in the middle of the stern and ran across the afterdeck to a cleat portside of the cockpit. He oozed out into the foot-deep cockpit, hoping the Romans couldn't see him. Abruptly, he burst from the cockpit's shelter and streaked across the six feet of open deck to whack at the line. He chopped frantically and the line snapped. A javelin thunked into the deck behind him. Joe dived back into the shallow cockpit.

The *Alice* was moving out now, far faster under power than the bireme. Joe made silent prayer for the helm to be centred. How far would those Roman javelins carry? He had to run forward and cut or take in the bow line before they breasted the midharbour pinnacle.

Spears still thunked into the *Alice's* woodwork. A poorly cast pilum clattered slatwise into the cockpit. The Romans would be casting off their own lines soon. Would he ever outrange those damned spears?

Abruptly, the *Alice's* diesel strained, gave a tremendous racking sneeze, and stopped. With a sinking feeling Joe realised what had happened. The slack in his own bow line was tangled in a stranglehold around the *Alice's* screw. Forgetting the spears, Joe dived for the after scuttle.

'Get the rifle, Cook. You Moors . . .' He remembered they didn't understand English. He turned to the *imam*. 'Fight! Tell them fight quick!'

Ma Trimble loomed huge and quivering in his path.

'Keep those damned girls out of the way!' He dived into his cubicle, searching for the pistol. *Damn it! I knew I'd face spears sooner or later. Why didn't I have some shields made?* The revolver wasn't under his pillow. Finally he remembered where he'd hidden it after Howie's crusade.

He scrambled for the after scuttle. The Moors were already on deck; javelins whizzed past them as they disdained cover to yell insults. A spear struck one in the shoulder. He jerked it out and cast it back before sitting to examine himself.

The *korax* unhinged from the bireme's stubby mast and struck the *Alice's* deck with a splintering crash. The spike in its tip nailed both ships firmly together. Marines surged across the portable gangway onto the *Alice*. The second Moor gave a falsetto shriek and charged, trying vainly to force his sword between their immense semi-cylindrical shields.

Short Roman swords flickered like serpents' tongues. The Moor was on his knees now. Joe emptied his pistol into Romans who still charged across the gangway. He ducked into the shallow cockpit to reload. A short sword struck the Moor on the back of the neck and in the corner of his mind Joe said a prayer for all men who die not for honour or patriotism, but because some s.o.b. tells them to.

The rifle cracked and another legionary fell off the bridge. Joe began firing again. Roman discipline was beyond belief. The pistol was empty again. He swung it, trying to knock the sword out of the hand which darted from behind that shield. The shield edge came up smartly under his chin— and that was the end of the the fight for Joe.

9

Up till now he hadn't really believed. He had plodded blithely along with some blind, Pollyanna-like faith that everything would turn out all right. The Moors had been a lackadaisical lot compared with these Romans. He studied them covertly through his eyelashes, pretending he was still unconscious. They had hard, curveless faces—all slabs and angles—with the humourless look of pure fanaticism.

Someone kicked him. He struggled to his feet and immediately a brass-knuckled fist knocked him down again. Romans passed like ants in an endless stream down the after scuttle and up the forward, inspecting and looting.

This is it, Joe thought. These slab and angle faced Romans would not be so easily bamboozled as Vikings and Moors. A hobnailed boot rolled him over again. '*Qui' e' ma'ister?*' the boot's owner asked. The scholarly corner of Joe's mind noted that even this early the Roman lower classes were dropping their s's and g's.

'*Ego sum*,' he answered.

'Not are—were,' the Roman corrected. He led Joe across the *korax* and Joe glanced briefly at the island. How could it lie there, primitive and peaceful, when his own world had just come crashing to an end? And where, he wondered briefly, was the caïque? But the Roman was whacking him across the buttocks with the flat of his sword. Joe stumbled off the end of the *korax*, onto the catwalk, and made his way aft to the poopdeck.

There, enjoying the bright morning sunlight, sat a man in a folding chair, behind a folding desk, on which lay a great many unfolded papers. The breeze kept fluttering the papers and he had them weighted down with sword, dagger, his gold collar, and his brass knuckles. With his left hand he slid pebbles in the slots of an abacus-like gadget of terra cotta while scribbling sums on a wax tablet with his right. From the look on his face, things weren't adding up. 'Now what?' he growled.

The marine explained.

'Speak Latin?' the man behind the desk asked.

'A little.'

'Where from?'

'America.'

'Where's that?'

'About 4000 Roman miles west of the Pillars of Hercules.'

'I'll bet,' the Roman grunted. 'What's your name?'

'Josephus Rate.'

'You don't look like a Jew.'

'I'm not. I'm an American. If it'll clarify things, my great grandfather was born in Brittania.'

The Roman fixed one unblinking barracuda eye on him.

'Others of my line came from Germania and Hibernia.'

'Quite a mongrel, aren't you?'

'You Romans aren't exactly pure any more.' From the other's pained look Joe knew he had struck a nerve.

The Roman gave him a long, hard stare, then barked an order. Joe found himself propelled back amidships. The oarmaster put him at one of the starboard top bank oars. At last he was getting firsthand knowledge of the question which plagued every scholar a century fore and aft of Mahan. His limp right hand was thrust into a manacle. An armourer riveted it shut, missing once with the hammer and skinning Joe's knuckle. The cuff fastened with a foot of chain to the heavy five manned oar. Joe was outboard, facing forward next to the oar-lock. Who said the Romans never invented anything, he wondered?

Greek and Phoenician penteconters needed skilled oarsmen—and a man couldn't learn to row in a day. With three men on each lower oar and five on the each upper, this quinquereme required only one oarsman to each. The other two or four faced each other and followed his stroke. The stroke man was not chained. Joe wondered if he was a trusted slave or working for wages.

They were an odd lot, ranging from a bluegum Nubian to several blond Scandinavian giants. Joe tried to guess the language. Here a Latin word cropped up, there a phrase in Greek koinê. It was beyond Joe. An artificial language, he guessed, like Legion French, the sort of bastard dialect which develops whenever strangers are thrown together.

He had finally succeeded in thoroughly and irremediably botching things up. And, he reflected, it was all his own fault. Why couldn't he have gotten out of here last night? Under jib and jigger the *Alice* would have been twenty miles away by now and with daylight he could have set the main.

Too tired! This was what happened to captains who could afford to get tired. He took a deep breath and tried to drive the mind sapping despair out of his body. What was he going to do? Mutiny?

That, he suspected, he would not do. He climbed on the narrow bench, standing as straight as the chain would permit. The *imam* was five oars ahead of him. Gorson was chained to an oar on the portside. The rest of the *Alice's* men were scattered throughout the lower bank.

What had happened to Ma Trimble and her girls? They would switch allegiance at a moment's notice anyway—why worry? He wondered how he would stand up under the strain of rowing. How would he take the oarmaster's lash?

He looked aft again. Gorson was sunk in apathy, his head resting on his oar. Raquel forced her way to the top of his unwilling mind. Ma Trimble's blondes were of this era and capable of looking after themselves. But Raquel—From where he sat amidships no female was visible. He squinted through the thole hole down at the *Alice*.

Roman *nautae* were fumbling helplessly with her running rigging. They had the jigger raised after a fashion, though its luff puckered and bagged like Maggie's drawers. Great snarls and Irish pennants festooned the mainmast. They had not fathomed the mysteries of the winch ratchet, nor had they managed to raise jib or mains'l.

Someone shouted and they cast off the *Alice's* stern line. A moment later they bunched in the bow and, ignoring the electric windlass, began hauling the *Alice* hand over hand toward the pinnacle which moored her bow. Not understanding the why of the chain locker's eye, they piled line in a great tangled heap atop the winch.

An expectant rustle ran through the oar benches. Better pay close attention, Joe decided. There was a double blatsnort from an offkey trombone. The anchor man on each oar began unlashing the oar behind him. Joe hurried with the lashings but he was too late.

CRACK! The noise numbed his eardrums like a pistol in a small room. He felt his shirt rip between his shoulder blades. That mad corner of his mind admired the skill of an oarmaster who could create such a devastating effect without harming his animals. He was still fumbling with the strange knots when the CRACK came again. It ploughed an inch-long furrow across the point of his shoulder blade.

He finally slipped the lashing. There was another flat blat and he stumbled hastily backward to avoid being crushed between his own oar and the bench. Someone began pounding a drum. After a couple of strokes Joe began to get the feel of the rise, one step forward, fall back on the bench.

The oar was clumsy as a telegraph pole. Most of its power came from inboard where the unchained oarsman guided the stroke, walking three steps fore and aft. He barked a single unintelligible word at Joe. On the next stroke Joe pushed harder.

Another discordant blat. They stopped, backing water with one reverse stroke. Joe pushed the wrong way, working against the four men.

CRACK! This time the lash bit deeper.

They rested, awaiting the next signal, and Joe glanced covertly at the man who held the whip, studying the greying, shaggy haircut, the jutting chin with its week-old growth of black beard, engraving this face in his memory. What had become of his detached historian's viewpoint? That ignorant clod was merely doing his job. Joe shrugged. The welts began to throb. His scholarly detachment departed, along with several of his boyish illusions.

The trumpet blatted and the drum began thumping again. Rise, push forward, fall back again—this time very slowly. There was a slight jerk and he guessed the hawser between the quinquereme and the *Alice* had gone taut. The drum thumped more rapidly.

They towed the *Alice* out of the horseshoe harbour and around the island. Joe burst into torrents of sweating. Once around the island, the full force of the wind hit them. They headed northwest, dead into it.

Even amid his distractions Joe found an instant to marvel over the change. It was at least fifteen degrees cooler outside the harbour. He was still sweating but the wind kept his clothes dry. What, he wondered, would happen if they suddenly stopped rowing? Probably pneumonia. But the galley showed no signs of stopping so he continued his rise, push forward, fall back on rubbery legs, wondering if the other oarsmen—Slaves was the word; he was a slave. Were the others as tired as he or would he harden to this life and become an unthinking rising, pushing, falling animal—another piston in the galley's enormous inefficient engine?

Though he had not noticed it, the drum had been slowing down. The galley alone was a rough go into the wind, and the *Alice's* external ballast and deep draft did not make for easy towing. They were still in sight of the island when, after four hours of suggesting and hinting, the quartermaster finally got his bit of information into the landlocked skull of his captain. Came a final despairing blat and oarsmen abruptly collapsed, leaving unshipped oars to dangle. Before Joe had time to worry about pneumonia he was unconscious.

Someone had him by the hair. He opened bleary eyes and recognised the man with the whip. *Must remember that face.* Someone was standing on the catwalk above them. It was the man who'd questioned him from behind a deskful of papers. 'Can you make that ship go?' the Roman asked.

Joe stared, still half asleep.

'Don't waste my time,' the Roman snapped. 'You had that ship moving without sails in the harbour. Can you do it again?'

Joe stared, trying to focus on the Roman. Why did the showoff have to wear polished armour at sea, aboard his own ship?

'Useless!' the Roman snapped to his quartermaster. 'Back to the island and beach it. Burn it and we can at least get something for the iron.'

Joe snapped out of his lethargy. They were going to destroy his only link with the past. Or was it the future? 'No!' he shouted. 'No, I can sail it. It's too valuable to burn. I can make you rich!'

The Roman gave him a contemptuous glance and strode off down the catwalk. Joe collapsed across the oar again.

Without the *Alice's* vacuum pump and still there was no hope of seeing the Twentieth Century again. Nor would his historian fraction ever see more of the ancient world than the inside of some prison where slaves were quartered during the winter months when navigation was dangerous. He was slipping off into dreamless, hopeless sleep when someone shook him again.

To hell with it! They'll wear me out and throw me overboard. Let them beat me to death right now. But the shaking wouldn't stop. There were clanks and hammerings. He opened his eyes in time to see a chiselled rivet head pop off the single manacle.

'Come on,' the armourer was saying in atrocious Greek, 'don't keep the *kybernetes* waiting.'

Walking down the catwalk, Joe suddenly realised what Christians meant when they spoke of being born again. He tried to attract Gorson's attention but the chief lay crumpled over his oar.

The Roman captain still sat in his folding chair.

'We are not magicians,' Joe began, 'but our arts require years of training. I'll need some of my men.'

'How many kinds of fool do you take me for?' the Roman snapped. 'You'll teach Roman sailors or go back to your oar.'

Joe's confidence evaporated. He glanced astern at the *Alice* and the island. They had drifted back toward it and were less than four miles away now. 'I don't know how much damage you've done,' he said. 'It may take time to get things working right. Can you set sail and tow us away before we ground?'

The captain shot a questioning glance at his oarmaster, who sputtered a rapid sentence in Greek. The captain nodded. 'We'll go back into harbour again. Will that suit you?'

'Well enough,' Joe agreed.

'And while you're being towed back you can give my men their first lesson in your devious barbarian arts. I'm going aboard too and see what your bucket looks like.'

Another beautiful plan shot to hell. Oh well, it was better than being chained to an oar. He thought guiltily about the others, the *imam* and old Dr. Krom . . . and Raquel?

Nautae hauled on the hawser and jumped aboard. Joe sprang after them and a moment later the captain, still in polished armour, came down a rope ladder. A striped sail bellied aboard the galley and *nautae* paid out the hawser slowly.

Joe went below, followed by the captain and six *nautae*. One look at the *Alice's* interior made him want to cast his manly inhibitions aside and weep. The Romans had gone through her like army ants, taking everything not nailed down and several things that were.

There was not a single bunk with a mattress in it. Every book, chart, binoculars, dividers, pencil, was gone from Joe's cubicle. Tools and spare parts were missing from Rose's engine lockers.

Cups, plates, pots, spoons, knives, and forks had disappeared from the galley, along with the stove lids. Not a can of food remained in stores. The lazarette had been emptied of the last grain of rye. Gorson and Cookie's empty food lockers were gone. Even the porthole curtains had departed.

'I can't run the ship this way,' Joe said.

'You'll run it this way or go back to your oar!'

'Then let's go,' Joe said, and turned to leave the ship.

The Roman captain lost his air of certainty. 'You want to be chained to that oar again?' he asked.

'Why promise what I cannot do? You've stolen too many pieces.'

The Roman bit his lip and pondered. 'Can you run it alone if I bring things back?'

'I don't know. Get every last scrap back aboard and I'll try.'

The Roman thought a moment. He suspected that if he could just understand some of this gadgetry it could be very useful. Burning her for iron, on the other hand, would scarcely pay his docking fees in Piraeus. 'Which things do you need?' he asked.

Joe shrugged. 'Each man in my crew has his own skill. I cast a horoscope and tell them which star to follow. They work the ship.'

The Roman's face was settling back into the planes and angles of Roman intolerence. 'And you alone cannot make this ship go?'

'I didn't say that,' Joe said hastily. 'But it will take longer. What do I *need*? How the hell should I know? I need everything. Do I get it or not?'

The other surveyed him a moment in frosty indecision. 'All right,' he finally grunted 'But none of your own men and no tricks.' He rattled orders in a Greek too fast for Joe and *nautae* began overhanding the hawser. Joe glanced at the electric winch and shrugged. Why run down batteries? After much heaving and grunting the *Alice* nuzzled up under the galley's stern. The Roman captain climbed up the ladder.

Joe glanced at the sun. Another couple of hours daylight, he guessed. Since losing the sextant he'd had no way to set his watch. He glanced at it.

Why, the dirty thieving sons of bitches!

It wasn't much of a watch but to Joe's father it had represented considerable sacrifice on the day his son graduated. In memory of this Joe had kept it long past the day when he could have afforded something better. He thought fleetingly of his father—how hard the old man had worked, how easily the world had swindled him out of his meagre earnings. And now the world had gotten away with his graduation present to his only son!

Joe squinted at the galley and decided it was time to stop seeing both sides of every question. He turned his attention to the six *nautae* who chattered to each other in some kind of Greek.

Jerking a peremptory thumb, he strode to the *Alice's* bow.

130

'Down this hole,' he growled. 'Don't pile the anchor line on deck, you miserable philosophers.' He poked a couple of feet through the deck eye and stood back. *Nautae* stared. 'Get on the ball!' Joe roared, and drove his fist into the nearest nose.

Blood spouted and the sailor dropped into a crouch. Joe stood erect, arms folded across his chest. The *nauta* knew a captain when he saw one. He shrugged and went to work.

The galley turned and lowered sail. Oars flashed raggedly as exhausted men took up the beat. The *Alice's* people were still chained to them. What was he going to *do*?

They would have to wait until the stores were back aboard. Trying not to worry about Raquel, he went below.

The Romans had lifted the floorboard over the engine. Joe began studying the maze of pipes and valves, trying to figure out the short cuts Rose had taken when he shut off the galley stove. Why, he wondered, weren't history teachers required to know more of practical mechanics?

They were nearly in the harbour now so he guessed he could safely open the valves which allowed sea water into the heat exchanger and out of the exhaust. How much fuel was left? The day tank glass showed half full, enough for two or three hours running. He opened the valve at its bottom and waited to see if anything around the engine started dripping. So far so good. The lifter bar was up. Better leave it that way until the engine was spinning. What shape were the batteries in? Would it start?

He looked about the tiny compartment and breathed a silent prayer of thanks. The can of starting ether was still there, one of the few things the Romans hadn't pilfered. Nothing was dripping so he decided to leave all valves open. Was everything right now? Water valve open, exhaust gate valve open, lifter bar up . . . The engine should roar into life as soon as he switched on the starting batteries and dropped the lifter. Forgetting anything?

Holy hell! Abruptly, he realised what was wrong. They would have made good their escape this morning if line hadn't fouled the screw. No wonder the galley hadn't been able to tow the *Alice*! How many hundred feet of line draped in tangled festoons from the yawl's screw?

A *tuba* blatted and he felt the *Alice* lose way. Moments later they tied to the pinnacle and the *Alice* was warped up alongside. The *korax* was lowered to her deck again and a working party started transferring the loot back. Joe spent the next couple of hours frantically sorting and directing packers to deposit things somewhere near their proper place. It would take weeks to get things where they belonged. He suspected the Romans were holding out everything small enough to hide.

Eventually the double column ceased flowing back and forth across the *korax*. Joe snatched a mattress and a couple of blankets and stuffed them into his cubicle. He was thinking guiltily about the *Alice's* men still chained to oars.

Morning came and his problems were still there. *Nautae* munched round loaves of bread. 'Where's mine?' Joe asked. They started to give him the stupid treatment again but something about the young man's stance made the mangle-nosed one reconsider. He produced Joe's loaf from the folds of his *himation*. Joe wolfed down his bun—much harder than he'd expected—and wondered if one was all the others had eaten. Probably. Roman efficiency would make a galley slave's breakfast indivisible and as small as the difference between life and death.

He had to do something soon or he would be back pulling an oar without another chance. No use teaching Romans the fine points of sailing into the wind. The Roman captain expected a miracle that could be accomplished only with the diesel. He turned abruptly to the *nautae* and stopped. He wanted to ask if there was a diver among them but he couldn't remember the Greek. Come to think of it, he didn't remember the word in Latin either. '*Scitisne natare?*' he finally asked. They looked Greek and Greeks used to skindive for sponges. The man whose nose he'd flattened seemed to be some kind of a leader. 'You,' Joe said. 'Down to the bottom and bring me a rock.'

He was given the stupid act again. It worried Joe. Maybe they really didn't understand Latin. But sweet reasonableness was not characteristic to commanders of this period. Joe pushed the man overboard.

The *nauta* hit the water with arms and legs going like windmills. A second later he came up gasping. 'Swim, damn it!' Joe growled. The *nauta* was putting on a good act. He choked and swallowed water before going down again. Several seconds passed this time before his head broke water and the Greek's pasty complexion finally convinced Joe. Disgustedly, Joe tossed a line. The Greek was too far gone to grab it.

'Everything happens to me,' he growled, and jumped in. A moment later he had the line secured around the unconscious *nauta* and those aboard dropped their stupid act long enough to pull them in.

It took several minutes of Holger-Nielsen pumping before the Greek finally coughed and vomited a half gallon of water along with his breakfast. 'Go back aboard the galley,' Joe said when the Greek sat up. 'Stay there and tell the skipper to send me a . . .' Damn it, what was the word for diver? '. . . someone who hunted sponge.' The *nauta* nodded sickly and vomited once more before crossing the *korax*.

Joe waited but there was no sign of a replacement for the waterlogged *nauta*. 'Damn them all,' he grunted and went to sorting the *Alice's* stores. Somewhere there had been a diving outfit. The air tanks were long since empty but with the faceplate Joe might be able to hack away a few strands of nylon between breaths. But where was the faceplate?

He found the tanks and regulator buried in a pile of gear dumped in the *Alice's* cockpit, but the face mask was still gone.

The more Joe thought about it the madder he got. He swung himself onto the *korax* and marched across, down the catwalk and aft to the quinquereme's poopdeck. 'Where's the *magister* of this bucket?' he roared.

The oarmaster appeared and rasped something in Greek. Joe stiffened his arms to keep from killing the man who'd whipped him. 'I defecate on your metaphysical tongue,' he said. 'Can't you speak Latin?'

'Somewhat better than you,' the oarmaster said sharply. 'And what's the idea of using up my men? You think they're cheap?'

The Roman captain erupted from the stern castle. 'I'll castrate the next man who awakens me!' he promised, then caught sight of Joe.

'Why doesn't a Roman keep his word?' Joe grated.

'And what do you mean by that?'

'I mean everything small enough to hide is hidden. If you want that ship to run, give it back!'

'What specifically do you want?'

'Everything. At the moment I'm looking for a face-plate.'

'A what?'

Joe tried to describe it. The Latin for glass didn't mean the kind you see through. What had they called mica? *Lapis specularis*! 'If I don't get it your thieving thugs have stolen a ship from you.'

The Roman captain sighed. The marines were Romans; if he couldn't keep them in hand he might as well open an artery. 'Fall in!' he trumpeted.

Seconds later he scowled at them. 'One article of loot is missing. You will fall out and return with full packs. You will march single file around the capstan. If this barbarian does not find the article he needs you will all swim home.

DisMISS!' the Roman spun sharply, still at attention. 'And you,' he said to Joe, 'will wait aboard the prize.'

To his own infinite surprise, Joe saluted. He turned bemusedly and ambled forward along the catwalk. Gorson was awake now. Joe caught his eyes but the chained chief's look was expressionless. Where were the women?

The sun was nearing noon before a work party clumped across the *korax* and deposited a small pile of odds and ends in the cockpit. The faceplate was there. His watch was not. So it be, he decided—a life for each jewel, a hundred for the hairspring. He turned to the *nautae* who watched. 'Give me a knife.'

The stupid act again.

'God damn you all! He rummaged through the pile again, and found one of Cookie's boning knives. Someone had apparently been trying to cut wire rope with it. Where in hell was the stone? Twenty minutes passed before he found it and another twenty in honing. He stripped, tied the knife to his wrist, and donned the faceplate.

The water was warmer than usual, and oddly murky. Tiny bubbles rose from the bottom. He remembered Dr. Krom and his test tubes. Was the old man still alive?

He pawed his way downward and was shocked to feel barnacles. When had the *Alice* been hauled out last? The water was ungodly murky. He could scarcely see his hand before the faceplate. He swam under the keel and swore, blurping a gob of water inside his faceplate as another barnacle snagged his back. He came up on the far side and breathed. No wonder he couldn't see; the *Alice* was in the quinquereme's shadow.

Resignedly, he climbed back aboard and crossed the *korax* again. The Roman captain was busy with lunch. 'Don't bother me,' he said. 'Tell him your troubles.'

Joe explained to the quartermaster.

'So what do you want me to do?' the quartermaster asked.

135

'Put a gang ashore. Warp her around until I can see.'

The quartermaster considered a moment. 'All right,' he grunted. 'Go back aboard so I can raise the *korax*.'

By the time the *Alice* was relocated, nearly two hours had passed. Joe dived sporadically, working by feel. The tightly wound nylon was not as hard to cut as he had expected.

And now the *Alice*, at least, was out from under the *korax*'s iron spike. All afternoon he racked his brains but no plan came to him. The pistol was not among the items returned. He wondered if they recognised it as a weapon or if it had gone overboard. The rifle was gone too. They'd had experience with the weird and wonderful weapons of barbarians. A rifle was not so far removed from a blowgun that Romans could not deduce its purpose.

The water was muddier now. Bubbles rose until each wavelet was capped with dirty brown foam like the dregs of a Bockfest. Dr. Krom must've seen something of this in his test tubes. Joe wondered if it were a periodic phenomenon or whether something unusual was abuilding.

From time to time he brought up strands of nylon, mainly to satisfy Roman curiosity and convince them he was not whittling holes to scuttle the yawl. The *nautae* remained on deck and didn't help him aboard when he came up for a rest.

Line had whipped round and round the shaft until the ball was bigger than the screw. The outer layers had been easy, for each blind stab had severed a strand. Closer to the shaft each miss dulled the knife. He tried once to get the *nautae* to sharpen another knife so he could alternate but they were putting on their stupid act again. Diving in the tepid water had done away with much of his stiffness from rowing but he'd only had that one small loaf to eat in the last twenty-four hours. When would be be fed again? It was late afternoon before he hacked the final twist and felt the wheel turn free. He surfaced and crawled wearily back into his clothes.

The five *nautae* watched him silently. Their dirty black headcloths and bloused up, topheavy *himations* gave them an odd, birdlike look, like hooded vultures. He went below, mentally running over the engine starting procedure again.

The sun had gone down but they would have moonlight in half an hour. He checked the valves again to make sure the *nautae's* curiosity hadn't sabotaged his arrangements. The engine was ready. Or was it? He ran through everything once more and finally, with a silent invocation to Mahan's ghost, threw the switch. The engine spun vigorously until he whanged over the lifter bar, then groaned nearly to a standstill. He was reaching for the ether when it suddenly roared into fullthroated life.

A glance at the ammeter showed how hungry the batteries were. He wondered about Rose's wind charger, then remembered there had been practically no wind inside the sheltered harbour. After a couple of tentative surges the diesel settled down to its steady racketing pound. Joe went on deck and threw in the forward clutch.

The *Alice* tugged at her stern line. He reversed and was satisfied that no line remained tangled. He pulled the lifter bar. In the sudden silence a sound came clearly from the quinquereme. A girl was screaming. The hooded vultures regarded him speculatively in gathering darkness. Joe found a length of nylon line.

He made it fast to the mainmast and tailed the strand aft, along one rail, tying it down with marline stops every yard or so. He tailed the line across the stern, up the opposite rail, up and around the mizzenmast on the same side, the back to the rail and almost to the mainmast again. There he tied an overhand knot before running the line aft through the mooring eye.

A light bobbed on the harbour's surface. It neared and Joe recognised the galley's longboat. Still in armour, the

Roman captain stumped aboard the *Alice*. He was backed up by a pair of particularly ugly marines. One of the oarsmen handed up a basket and lit another torch before handing up the one in the longboat's bow. 'Ready?' the captain asked.

'I can make the ship move. Where were you going yesterday?'

'Piraeus.'

'How far?'

'Five hundred stadia.'

Eight to the mile, Joe thought, and calculated rapidly. To keep the Roman from disbelieving him, he doubled his estimated time. 'If we leave right now, I can have you docked tomorrow afternoon.'

The hooded vultures were gobbling bread from the basket. Joe kicked them sprawling and helped himself to three loaves.

'One apiece,' the Roman captain snapped.

'They'll get their share when they work for it!' Joe snapped back. 'Are you ready?'

The Roman decided not to make an issue of it.

'Have them cast off their stern line.' While the Roman shouted orders Joe uncleated the line which tethered the *Alice's* bow to the galley and bent it onto his previously strung line.

'Cast off and ready,' the Roman said. 'What makes all the noise?'

'Have you seen the oil which flows from the earth and makes burning springs?'

'Yes, near Sinai.'

'The noise of its burning pushes the ship.' Joe threw the switch to demonstrate and the arm diesel started immediately. He backed slowly around the pinnacle taking care not to foul the stern line. The moon rose over the jagged crater top and he hoped his manœuvre would come off properly before it got too light. 'Douse the torch,' he said.

'Like hades I will! You must think I trust you.'

'All right,' Joe growled. 'But tell those useless sons of bitches to stand back astern and sing out when that line comes taut. I don't want to tear something out by the roots getting under way.'

The Roman captain condescended the tremendous gap which separated him from a *nauta* and relayed Joe's order. The *Alice* had drifted backward until her stern was within a length of the galley's bronze ram. There were a couple of hundred feet of nylon between them and Joe had been keeping a careful eye on its floating mass lest the *Alice* foul her screw again.

'Here we go,' he said, and shoved the lever into forward. The *Alice* gathered way rapidly. Joe made sure she was headed for the harbour mouth and would clear the pinnacle, then squatted in the foot-deep cockpit to study the tachometer and ammeter. 'If you're interested . . .' he hinted. The Roman knelt beside him. The marines fingered their swords nervously and stood on either side of their chief.

'Let me know when it comes taut,' Joe yelled at the hooded vultures. At that moment it did. There was a sputter like a string of wet firecrackers as marline stops tore loose along the rail. Line whiplashed over Joe's back where he knelt with the Roman commander. Marines and *nautae* gave startled yelps.

Joe had thought the closing loop would whip them overboard, but he'd underestimated the power and stretch of nylon. The *Alice* took up the full dead weight of the galley and shuddered. The line stretched its full twelve per cent.

The slipknot closed before vultures and marines had time for another yell. The vultures made strange sucking sounds as their insides burst and splattered over the *Alice's* deck.

The two marines had been standing a foot lower in the cockpit—they merely lost their heads.

Joe stared. He hadn't imagined it was going to be so messy. The Roman captain took in the situation almost as quickly as Joe, but not quickly enough to duck the steel lever Joe wrapped around his fine Roman head.

Bisected bodies jerked and quivered about the *Alice's* stern. Thanking Mahan the torch had gone overboard, Joe corrected course. They were just passing through the harbour mouth. He stumbled and cursed and kicked a pair of legs. They skidded overboard, dragging bloody viscera with them.

He wondered if anyone aboard the galley knew what had happened. They'd find out soon enough. He throttled down. How much fuel could he save without slowing enough to encourage some inquisitive soul to haul in the tow line?

The Roman captain groaned and stirred. Joe did things with short pieces of line. Then he snapped the end of the main halliard to the line joining the Roman's wrists.

The Roman came to. He tried to sit up as Joe began cranking the winch. He pronounced several words Joe had never heard before as the halliard came taut and began dragging him across the deck. 'What do you expect to gain by this?' he demanded.

Joe continued cranking until the Roman was lifted into a sitting position. With feet lashed to the bottom of the mizzen mast and wrists over his head, the Roman could sit but was forced off balance if he tried to stand and lower his arms. When Joe was sure his captive wasn't going anywhere he throttled down and began hauling in line as the galley coasted up to the deep drafted yawl. It drifted within fifty feet of the *Alice* before its speed matched that of the idling diesel.

What was going on aboard the galley? He waited tensely but no face peered down over the bow. With an uneasy glance at the bronze ram which pointed straight at the

Alice's screw, he cracked the throttle another notch. Now what?

They were a mile south of the island by now and the wind was offshore. One less worry. He was going to have to attract an audience. The Romans had stolen the trouble light along with everything else but he thought he'd seen a marine bring it back.

God must have been on his side, Joe decided, for it lit when he plugged it in. He snaked the cord back up on deck and hooked the caged lamp between the Roman's wrists.

'Hail them,' Joe said. 'Good and loud. Tell them to send my people back. You might also mention that if that galley unships one oar I'll sink it immediately.'

'And what do I get out of this deal?'

'If my people are alive and well you might live. If not I'll vivisect you.'

'Won't work,' the Roman snapped.

Joe considered the Roman a moment, then kicked him where it would do the most good. The ropes would not let the Roman bend double. He writhed and twisted like a maimed snake, and after a moment vomited. 'You don't understand,' he explained. 'Those bloodthirsty pirates wouldn't give a plugged *drachma* to ransom the whole Roman Empire.'

'Whose life would they value?'

The Roman thought a moment. 'The quartermaster's a Roman too. But maybe the oarmaster.'

Joe reached for the light between the Roman's wrists and cursed when he burnt his fingers trying to unscrew it. Incredibly, there was still no one looking down at them over the galley's bow. Were they all asleep? No, there had been a murmur of voices somewhere aboard the larger ship. Abruptly, a man screamed. His voice rose slowly through soprano and ended with an abrupt rabbit-like whistle.

Joe grabbed the Roman by the forelock and they faced

each other in the moonlight. 'If that's one of my people,' Joe promised, 'you are going to make several noises like that. Even then, I may not let you die.'

The Roman said something short and pungent which Joe didn't understand. Joe pulled a belaying pin from the mizzen ring and brought it down sharply on the Roman's kneecap. When the Roman had caught his breath Joe began a steady gentle tapping on the broken kneecap. 'All right,' he finally gasped. 'What do you want?'

Joe spun the wheel hard right and paid out line. When the *Alice* had drifted around broadside to the galley and headed in the opposite direction he declutched. 'Now yell. Tell that quartermaster and oarmaster to get over here in the skiff, alone, and on the double.'

'I don't know whether I can make them come alone,' the Roman hedged.

Joe began tapping on the kneecap again. The Roman began shouting. Minutes passed before the rope ladder tumbled down from the galley's stern castle and moonlight silhouetted one man climbing down into the skiff. 'Why only one?'

'I don't know. I told them both to come.' Joe hefted the belaying pin. 'I *did*,' the Roman insisted. They sat in uneasy silence until the skiff bumped beneath the *Alice's* stern.

A cloaked and hooded figure tossed up a painter. Joe cleated it and extended his left arm. As the man grasped it and swung up on deck Joe jerked. He brought the belaying pin down smartly on the other man's neck.

The oarmaster came to dangling back to back with the Roman.

'Where's the quartermaster?' Joe asked.

The oarmaster gave a short hard laugh. 'Dead,' he said. 'One of your trollops did him in a few minutes ago.'

'Which one?'

'The blackheaded one that kept herself so filthy no man

142

would touch her—until Harpalus got suspicious and caught her smearing herself in fish and seagull blood.'

A great light burst in Joe's mind. So that explained the gamy stink. Whenever things got dangerous Raquel copied the skunk and kept her person unclean but inviolate. He laughed involuntarily. But now she was in real danger! 'Yell back and tell them not to harm her!'

'Not on your life,' the oarmaster grunted. 'Old Harpalus deserved a cleaner death than she gave him.'

Joe remembered the welts on his shoulders. 'Have you ever felt a whip?' he asked.

'Yes, damn you!' the oarmaster replied in his Greek-tainted Latin. 'I've been a slave in my time.'

Joe hooked the light between their wrists. He cranked the main halliard winch until they dangled, swinging gently through the catenary arc which suspended them from maintop to mizzen butt. 'Tell them to get my people over here in one piece.' He tapped the Roman on the knee-cap again.

The Roman started yelling orders, and after the oar-master had considered the situation for a moment he joined in.

There was hammering aboard the galley. Manacles being unriveted, Joe guessed. 'Now hear this,' he said. 'All hands report on board immediately.'

Minutes passed and no one came. Joe picked up the be-laying pin. They started yelling again.

Still nothing happened. Maybe he should have taken more hostages before showing his hand.

Then there was a faint splash amidships and Joe spun in horror. He'd known these Greek swabbies were divers —why hadn't he been prepared for something like this? They were probably all around the ship now. And he hadn't so much as a knife at hand!

10

He crept forward toward the sound of splashing. A head popped up and Joe raised the belaying pin.

'Permission to board sir?' the head asked. Joe released breath in an explosive sigh. Gorson had swum around to the enlisted men's side. He clambered over the rail, faced aft, and saluted. Then he faced Joe and saluted again. 'Good to see you, sir,' the chief said.

'Mr. Rate,' the chief asked, 'aren't we going to show the flag?'

The question took Joe by surprise. 'Quite right,' he said after a pause. 'See to it.'

As Gorson turned Joe saw fresh welts across the bos'n's back. There was also a crease across his head where the whiplash had gouged a furrow and reopened his mangled ear.

The bos'n found the flag stuffed in a pile of blankets. He was running it up when two more heads bobbed up on to the enlisted men's side. 'Permission to board, sir?' Villegas asked. Freedy followed him. As they faced aft and saluted Joe began to understand what power these ceremonials had over the minds of men.

While Villegas was rowing back for a load of non-swimmers heads popped up. Rose, Cookie and Guilbeau climbed dripping over the enlisted men's side and saluted. As befitted a civilian, Lapham came over the officer's side and faced aft, seeming to be all knees and elbows. He blinked rapidly and blew his nose before facing Joe. 'Ready for duty, sir,' he said in a strange quavering voice.

Another head popped up along the enlisted men's side. It was Raquel. Unbound black hair lay wetly over her back and shoulders. The coarse woollen dress clung beautifully.

'¿Permiso to boar', sair?' she asked.

Joe swallowed and returned her salute. Raquel glanced briefly at the dangling Roman and his oarmaster, then turned back to Joe with an enigmatic look.

Joe had forgotten them. He went forward and unlatched the winch until they could sit again.

The Roman studied Joe with new respect. 'What is that bloody rag you worship?' he asked.

'A symbol,' Joe explained, 'of the slow-footed, butter-fingered, bungling Great White Father whose stupidity we curse daily.'

'A strange way to worship one's gods.'

'Yes, isn't it? Takes an experience like this to understand what's really going on when you stand at attention while the squadron's father image runs up a bloody rag.'

'Barbarians,' the Roman muttered.

To Joe's surprise, Dr. Krom was still alive. The old man wept without shame as he faced aft. Ma Trimble was lifted aboard with much grunting and wheezing. She stood a moment facing aft in silent awe. 'Sonny,' she asked, 'what are the extra stars for?'

'What about your girls?' Joe asked. 'I've seen eight or ten so far.'

Chins, breasts and abdomens quivered as Ma Trimble laughed. 'Stop worrying sonny,' she said. 'Most of your swab jockeys've settled down with one or another. The odd girls decided they'd rather take their chances with the Romans. Of course, I can call 'em over.'

'Oh no!' Joe said quickly. Thank God the *Alice* wouldn't be quite so crowded now.

There were nineteen persons aboard: himself, Gorson,

Guilbeau, Cook, Villegas, Schwartz, and Freedy. Raquel was there, along with Ma Trimble and seven of her girls. Ten men and nine women. Who was the odd man? Twenty-four hours ago Joe would automatically have considered himself the odd man.

Cookie was the only man without a companion. Even Dr. Krom was paying archaic, old world courtesies to Ma Trimble's trembling bulk.

'How come no girl?' Joe asked the gaunt Tennessean.

'Already got a wife.'

'She'd never know,' Villegas hinted.

'I would,' Cook said.

Joe regarded him with new respect.

Red Schwartz had latched onto one of the more spectacular blondes. 'All here but one,' he said.

Joe also remembered McGrath. 'Yea,' he said glumly. All but one. But it wasn't quite true. The *imam* had not been of the *Alice's* original company but Joe had a special affection for the old man—an affection which extended to the young Moors who had so lightheartedly accepted their new master. They had died for the *Alice*.

The *imam's* aged heart had beaten its last in the galley's under bunk. Chained three oars aft, Dr. Krom had seen this part discarded from the galley's immense, inefficient engine and wondered if he would be next.

Joe unsnapped the main halliard from his captives' wrists. 'One of my men is dead,' he said. They sat, not bothering to look at him. Joe worried at their bonds with a pair of scissors. Cookie went below for a knife.

Eventually the line parted. The hostages stood unsurely, rubbing their swollen wrists. The Roman's arrogance was returning with his circulation. 'A Roman has kept his word,' he sneered. 'Now we shall see if a barbarian keeps his.'

Joe fingered a welt high on his shoulder and wondered how many stripes it had taken to still the old *imam's* heart.

'I keep my promises,' he said, and pushed them overboard. They were still tethered to the mizzen mast and the line was short enough to hold their feet out of water. After some preliminary splashing they arched themselves and held their heads above water by grasping their ankles.

Joe surveyed them dispassionately, noting with interest how the planes and angles of the Roman's face blurred into new and softer lines as he understood he was about to die.

The moon hung low in the west now. Almost morning, Joe guessed. The galley still drifted with all oars shipped, a hundred yards away. Both ships had drifted until the island lay three or four miles east. The hostages' heads drooped lower until only their faces were out of water. A wavelet washed over and they coughed, struggling to raise their heads for a clean breath. Cookie came on deck with the knife.

It was over. He had his ship back and most of his people. 'Cut them loose,' he grunted.

Cookie slashed. They struck out for the galley, swimming clumsily because they were still bound together by the feet. Dr. Krom appeared beside Joe. 'I don't wish to interfere,' he said deferentially, 'but we really should be leaving. Do you remember those test tubes?'

Joe nodded absently. The two swimmers were halfway to the quinquereme. Abruptly, they stopped swimming and started yelling.

'Leaving? Oh yes,' Joe remembered. 'Rose, light 'er off.'

'Yes sir!' Rose twiddled topside controls and the warm diesel started immediately.

Things were finally happening aboard the Roman ship. Oars unshipped and stroked rapidly toward the two swimmers. Joe threw in the forward clutch and spun the wheel, idling the *Alice* gently upwind so they could make sail. Dead ahead the island silhouetted in the faint beginnings of dawn. 'Look,' Dr. Krom said. A thin tendril of smoke issued from the crater.

But Joe was looking elsewhere. The quinquereme had quickstroked to full speed. Nearing the two swimmers, she tossed out a spar for them to cling to and raced on without missing a stroke. The bronze ram was less than a hundred feet away, aimed straight for the *Alice's* midships. Joe rammed the throttle home.

He thumbed his nose as the *Alice* walked away from the undermanned galley. Once more he was heading south, toward the mouth of the Aegean. One right turn at the Sea of Crete and they wouldn't stop till they reached the Azores. Saving the diesel for emergencies, he could outrun anything the Romans could send against him.

Water tanks were still full, thanks to the Roman ignorance of pumps. He wondered what would have happened if they had discovered all that wine. While the *Alice's* men traced out lines and undid the Roman snarls in standing and running rigging, Cookie squared away the galley and put girls to grinding flour.

They were a mile ahead now and the galley was turning toward the oarmaster and captain, who still clung to a floating spar.

Raquel hadn't said a word to Joe since boarding, yet some instinct told him their relationship had changed. Bloodthirsty savage, he'd called her. How could he have known what lay so close beneath his own civilised exterior?

Then the engine stopped.

The quinquereme was completing its pickup, about a mile and a half behind them. Joe wondered if the engine's noise could carry that far upwind. His question was answered when the immense striped sail dropped from its yard and bellied. The bronze ram lifted and began throwing twin wings of spray. 'Make sail!' Joe shouted.

'Be a few minutes yet,' Gorson answered. 'Those sons of bitches unrove the mainsheet.'

Dawn was a little brighter now and the island was

clearly outlined some five miles astern. 'None too soon,' Dr. Krom was saying. 'Look at that smoke.'

Joe went to see what had happened to the engine. 'Day tank ran empty,' Rose explained.

'I didn't know how to fill it,' Joe apologised.

'The engine drives the transfer pump.'

Joe began to worry. 'And without fuel to start the engine you can't pump fuel into the day tank to run the engine to . . .'

Rose laughed. 'I'll drain a cupful somewhere.' He grabbed a wrench and crawled deep into the *Alice*'s bilges. 'Don't worry,' his muffled voice came back. 'I'll find a plug soon.'

The galley had closed to less than a mile. Joe studied its bow wave and wondered if the *Alice* could outrun this light drafted vessel downwind. If it came to that the *Alice* could come about and tack until the oarsmen were exhausted.

'How much longer with that sail?'

'Any minute,' Gorton said cheerfully. The galley was making a good nine knots now and the plume of smoke which rose directly behind her gave Joe the momentary impression of a destroyer preparing to ram at flank speed. He was starting down the after scuttle again when he heard the starting motor grind. The diesel coughed raggedly and the glass tube on the side of the day tank began filling. He went on deck to see what the galley would try.

'Not going to conk out again, is she?'

'If she does I'll turn Christian,' Rose promised.

The galley was within three hundred yards, gaining rapidly. Joe opened throttle and headed crosswind to take the weather gauge. Instantly, the sail brailed up and oars flashed as the galley turned. But the *Alice* was faster now and had no difficulty staying on the larger ship's stern. He caught a glimpse of the Roman captain, livid with rage as he shouted orders.

149

A catapult twanged and the stone splashed short.

This is ridiculous, Joe thought. He didn't want to waste fuel playing tag, yet the Roman wouldn't give up. The quinquereme was more solidly built than that Scowegian dragon ship. Joe might get the worst of it in a ramming match. To hell with it. He'd lead them off cross wind for a while, then set every stitch.

Another stone plunked short of the *Alice*. Joe cracked the throttle a trifle wider. 'Look!' Dr. Krom was pointing at the island, now dead ahead.

It reminded Joe of the Bikini movie. A visible shock wave moved through the clear morning air. A mile high pillar of smoke was already beginning to mushroom. How long before the tsunami reached them?

'All hands below!' he screamed at the spellbound deck force. 'Dog everything tight!' He pushed Dr. Krom through the scuttle and dived after him. Thank God they hadn't set sail! And the *Alice*, at least, was heading into it. 'In your bunks,' he yelled. 'Shut it off, Rose.'

The shock wave struck. There was no sound, just a feeling like the end of the world. Somewhere in the loudest silence he had ever known Joe heard a tinkle of broken glass.

There were ominous creakings and groanings, a hum which ended with a snap like an overturned guitar string. *If that's the backstay we need a mast.* The nearest suitable timber would be in Gaul. How many weeks to find and shave it down? No, by Mahan—the Bible mentioned cedars in Lebanon. But there wasn't fuel even to reach there.

The tsunami struck—a vertical wall of water which poured over the bow before the yawl could lift. Water poured through the slide behind him. Floorboards tilted slowly beneath his feet and he hung from the ladder. Girls screamed. The bow raised slowly, majestically skyward. Joe surveyed the wriggling mass below him and wondered why in hell they hadn't gotten in their bunks.

He heard water gurgling down the cockpit's self-bailing drains. The *Alice* came to an even keel and after a moment he opened the scuttle and scrambled on deck. The others streamed behind him and surveyed the turbulent, mud-coloured sea. There was neither splinter nor corpse of the Romans.

He turned ruefully to Dr. Krom. 'I see why you wanted to leave.'

The old man grinned, looking suddenly young. 'All my life I have lived with fear. First, it was the simple fear of starvation. Then came Hitler and new fears. All my life I have fought fear, seeking only to align myself with the lesser evil. Did you know the Communists also tried to buy me?'

What kind of confession was the old man leading up to?

'Freedom began the day I realised you were in command —that I could in no way influence events.' The old man smiled inwardly. 'To be a leader is always to be alone. Chained to an oar, I suddenly knew I was free—for the first time in my life. I knew the island would explode but I could not act so I did not care.'

Ma Trimble crowded up. 'Quite a band, sonny,' she said. 'Did you shoot off one of them atomiser things?'

Dr. Krom laughed and probed layers of fat with his fore-finger, poking in the general direction of Ma Trimble's ribs. 'Do you realise,' he asked Joe, 'that this blithe spirit has never heard of Hitler, Stalin, or Krushchev?'

Ma Trimble gave the scientist a kittenish glance and they moved off together.

The island was visibly changed. The mushroom had torn and was streaking over the *Alice*. The wind blew due south and deposited a fine ash over the *Alice* and the surrounding sea.

'Make sail,' Joe said. 'First reef until things settle down.'

It was nearly noon before they sighted land, ten degrees off the starboard bow. Joe reflected a moment. The Roman had been heading due west for Athens. They were possibly fifty miles south of that position now. He studied the inadequate pilot chart and cursed. Here he was, a historian professor travelling through the islands where so much of the western world's history had been made. Which was this? Was it the Paros which shuttled back and forth between Athens and Persia so many times? Could it be Naxos, where the god Dionysius picked up Ariadne after Theseus stood her up? Maybe it was Amorgus, where the Roman emperors sent their poor relations, or Kinaros, famous only for its artichokes. It couldn't be Kos, birthplace of that father of quacks, Hippocrates, or he'd have run aground long ago.

'Freedy,' he yelled, 'fire up the fathometer.'

'Two hundred fathoms,' Freedy reported a moment later.

Joe slapped a hand to his forehead and went below to the chart again. He decided to head south and try to thread his way out of this cluster of Cycladean islands. Even if he had fantastic luck to catch a fisherman, these smaller islands changed names every twenty years. Every other one was Iraklía, Herákleon, Herculaneum, or some such thing, all named after the omnipresent hero. Cape Malea, the southernmost tip of the Peloponnese, couldn't be more than another fifty miles south. And if the Roman had been heading west for Athens this morning, it must be at least a hundred miles west.

They rounded the island, whatever it was, and two hours later another appeared. Joe took the BuShip's name in vain. He could be three different places in the Aegean and still see two islands this far apart on this course. Damn the navy's meaching economy with charts! If he ever got back he'd write letters and damn the promotions.

Things were finally shipshape again. Not as shipshape as they had been, for all her arms and many other bits of the *Alice* were gone forever. From now on, Joe decided, he'd keep plenty of sea room. If the wind held and if all his other guesses were right, they'd clear the passage between Kíthera and Andikíthera just about daybreak. The next obstacle in their westward run would be Sicily.

The *Alice* galloped along on a broad reach under all plain sail. There had been disturbances and tidal waves throughout the day but it seemed to be over now. The *Alice*'s people were tired unto stumbling. They'd had several hours less sleep than Joe during the last forty-eight. Tired as he was, he was still the freshest man aboard.

'All hands sack out,' he said. 'I'll take the wheel.' He wanted to steer awhile—not to spare the crew so much as to be alone. When had he last had an interval of peace and quiet? He needed to think. This time travel business: there was something odd—well, it was all odd, but there was something even more than peculiar about it. He had thought it was the lightning and the still. Thank Mahan the Romans had brought back all the parts for the still . . . But something else came into it.

Lightning, yes. And the copper coil inside the still's vacuum chamber obviously had something to do with their jumps. But what else? If it were this simple every moonshiner would have ended up in the Roman army. There had to be another factor—something which existed only aboard the *Alice*. The standing rigging might serve as some sort of antenna. Even though not connected with the still, there might be some resonance between them.

Assuming time travel was an electromagnetic phenomenon—but how did he know there wasn't some entirely new form of energy involved? To dislocate an object in time must require an enormous expenditure of energy. That was where the lightning came in. What else? Radio? Freedy hadn't turned it on since they'd skipped back to an era without transmitters.

The moon rose and silhouetted the *Alice*. It was a clear, cloudless night and the horizon betrayed no hint of land.

It would have been nice to check his reckoning with the fathometer and make sure they were in the deeps off northern Crete but he hadn't the heart to wake Freedy.

Fathometer . . . By Mahan, that was it! Joe thought back carefully, reconstructing the events preceding each time jump. Each time the still had been set up; each time lightning had struck. But what had been the triggering factor? The fathometer! How, Joe wondered, could a sonic echo from its transducer heterodyne with whatever lightning was feeding through the still's coil produce the time travel effect? Whatever it was, it was beyond him. But it seemed to work. How could he reverse it?

If he set up the still and the fathometer and waited for another lightning flash, according to past experience, he wouldn't be home—he'd be another thousand years backward, about the time of the Trojan war. A hundred years before Solomon would get around to building his temple. Good God, what a chance . . . Joe sighed and pulled the *Alice* back on course. His first obligation was to his people and ship. If he ever got them home . . .

Gorson came on deck, yawning and stretching. 'Still two-thirty degrees?' he asked.

Joe nodded. 'If you spot any small islands, try to keep them astarboard.'

'By the way,' Gorson asked, 'what became of those Roman swabbies you had aboard?'

'They died.'

'All at once?'

Joe explained briefly about the looped hawser, then went below before Gorson could ask any more questions. How had be been able to do such things? His one undergraduate adventure had been the time he'd organised an anti-vivisection campaign and the biologists had landed on him like a ton of tormented tomcats .He felt his way through the darkened galley, marvelling at his own bloodthirstiness, admitting to himself that it had taken no great effort of will to perform this *auto da fé*. He remembered the horror with which he'd watched Raquel carve her initial in the Viking woman. Oh well. . . . He closed the door to his cubicle and turned on the light. After staring at the narrow, monastic bunk for a moment he sat on it and took off his shoes. 'What the hell were you expecting?' he muttered, and flipped the light out.

Dawn brought one of those bright sunny days when sails draw well and seagulls sing hymns to the sun—when porpoises, filled with *joie de vivre*, crisscross the bow and startled anchovies waste millions of tailpower frothing Homer's wine-dark sea. Cookie fried over a hundred rye pancakes—light, fluffy ones, thanks to some yeasty miracle —and though the butter was long gone, he had produced a sweet syrup, vaguely reminiscent of dried apricots.

Guilbeau was steering. Joe, after a glance at a morning worthy of young King David's harp, decided to hold his meeting on deck. He reviewed the time travel business and explained his hypothesis of the night before.

Freedy pursed his little mouth. 'How do we keep from going back in the past?'

'A good question,' Joe said. 'My guess is it takes power to drive anything out of its own time and that no matter how far away, that person or thing must always have an affinity for his position in time. Perhaps if the same process which dislocated him in the first place were repeated, but without power. . . .'

Lapham's Adam's apple bobbed several times. 'You mean the lightning?'

'Right,' Joe said. 'It was the still and, I think, the fathometer which got us in this fix, coupled with a couple of googol watts from a lightning discharge.'

Dr. Krom broke in excitedly. 'Let's try it—what can we lose?'

'Nothing we haven't already lost,' Schwartz said.

No one else objected, so Joe said, 'Gorson, you and

Cookie set up the still. Try to get everything like it was when we tangled with those Vikings off Catalina or Iceland or wherever.

'Freedy, make sure your gear's all there. Whatever you do, don't turn anything on!

'Rose, how are the batteries?'

'Half charge,' the engineman said. 'If the breeze holds and the windmill doesn't give out they'll be up in another day.'

'Everyone spend the day thinking over my theory. How many things can go wrong? After you come up with your objections I'll spring mine. If that doesn't scare you to death we'll throw the switch tomorrow.' He glanced automatically at his wrist and remembered his watch had gone down with the Romans. *Damn them; I might have been willing to let them live if it hadn't been for that.*

Raquel appeared beside him. 'You expect more trouble?' she asked.

'No,' Joe said, 'but I didn't expect to get out of television range of San Diego the day I sailed. Incidentally, how much English do you understand nowadays?'

Raquel shrugged. 'Your language is like the Viking tongue but I think it is worse. I still know only a few words.'

Villegas must have filled her in about the meeting, Joe guessed. Like every Latin gentleman, he preferred blondes and had set up bunkkeeping with one. Still, Joe felt an obscure discomfort and wished the great lover would keep away from Raquel. Not that Joe had any intentions, honourable or otherwise, but . . . He couldn't make up his mind just what he was butting.

The day wore on and no sight of land. Where were they? He was sure he'd passed Cape Malea by this time. How could he have managed that without sighting land? They'd be passing across the Ionian Sea's lower end soon, maybe already. He wondered how it would be for pirates, remembering that Julius Caesar had been taken and held for ransom here.

They had roast goat that afternoon. Surprisingly like venison, Joe decided. They had been horribly short of fats and rye bread dipped in hot tallow was delectable. The *Alice* was still well fixed for rye and meat but the island had contributed little or nothing in the way of greens, thanks to the same goats they were now eating. Joe ran his tongue over his teeth and wondered if it was imagination that made them feel slightly loose. How long before someone blossomed out with a genuine case of scurvy?

The still was ready. Radio and fathometer were still complete, if only because the Romans hadn't been able to imagine the cost of a power transistor. Joe turned in and threshed about in his bunk. Chances were when he got everything set up and threw the switch, nothing would happen. If something did there were about eighteen thousand things that could go wrong. The first jump had taken them from the Pacific to the Atlantic; the second had landed them in the Aegean. The reverse should take them back home—maybe.

He flipped on the light for a look at his watch. Damn it, would he never remember it was gone? He climbed wearily into his pants and hoped there would be some burnt rye in the coffee pot. If the fire hadn't died down in the range it might even be warm.

Lights were on and all hands sat up waiting in the galley. 'What time is it? Why's everybody up?'

'Homesick, sonny,' Ma Trimble said. 'Everybody's waiting for you to get off the pot.'

Joe stumbled toward the coffee pot which, thank Mahan, was full. Somewhere in the back of his mind had lurked the hope that with warm bunks and carnal satisfactions the *Alice's* crew would not be in such a hurry to get home. As the only historian aboard he had, he realised now, been indulging in wishful thinking. 'Hasn't anyone any objections?' he asked.

Silence.

'Well,' he continued, 'the first jump took us from off California to somewhere between Norway and Iceland. The next one dumped us in the Aegean. Why? Maybe we hang in limbo while the Earth revolves beneath us.' He shrugged. 'Anyway, each jump has moved us east. Now take a look at the map. If this next jump proves true to form the *Alice* is going to have one damn rough time sailing down Mt. Ararat.'

Shocked silence.

'But we got everything all ready to go,' Cookie finally protested.

'Okay,' Joe said, 'if everybody's willing, so am I. But remember, the biggest deserts on Earth lie due east. The Golden Horde of Fu Manchu couldn't dig a canal across the Gobi.'

There was silence for another moment; then Dr. Krom protested, 'But do you *know*?'

'Of course not,' Joe snapped. 'I'm guessing like everyone else. What time is it, anyway?'

'About dawn,' Gorson said. 'Guilbeau, relieve Schwartz.'

The Cajun nodded and climbed into his peacoat.

'Batteries at full charge,' Rose suggested.

A faint hint of daylight glimmered through the porthole. Joe didn't want to jump. He was haunted by the suspicion that he was forgetting something very important. He needed more time to think. Maybe he could get Freedy to check over the electronics gear again. He was trying to think up a reason to stall when Schwartz's raucous voice yelled. 'Land!'

Ten seconds later all hands stared at a rocky promontory off the starboard bow. Where in blazes were they? Joe was willing to bet his commission they'd passed Cape

Malea. This couldn't possibly be Sicily. He studied the point and wondered how far out that rocky spine would shoal. If the *Alice* headed any farther south she'd be sailing by the lee. Nothing for it but to haul everything in close and jibe.

'Want a sounding?' Freedy asked. 'I can turn on the fathometer.'

'With everything set up for a jump? Hell, no.'

They hauled in the mainsheet and were wrestling with the spinnaker pole when Joe first saw it come streaking from behind the point. The ship was light and carried a single bank of oars. 'Liburnian,' he grunted. Caeser used them for despatch boats. A second galley came from behind the point and shot towards the *Alice*.

'Dammit,' Gorson moaned, 'The s.o.b.'s must crawl from under every flat rock.'

Freedy stuck his head up through the companionway. 'You sure it's deep enough here?' he asked.

Joe gauged the wind against the quick-stroking Liburnians. 'We're in deep enough,' he said. 'Turn on the fathometer.'

11

Howard McGrath had not been having it easy. The night before the *Alice* had been taken by the Roman ship, he and Lillith had escaped in the caïque, but right now, with the wind abeam, the little vessel was about as stable as a bicycle. Out of bits of cordage they had finally rigged a couple of slings which permitted him and Lillith to dangle rapidly varicosing buttocks outboard of the windward gunwale while steering with the sheet rather than the lashed sweep.

After several eternities they reached Piraeus and brailed up sail. There being no proper thwarts, Howie had been at something of a loss until Lillith stood facing forward with her pair of oars and taught him how to row. In the hour and a half it took them to make land he felt circulation returning little by little to his cinctured lower extremities.

Instinct guided Lillith away from the moles where customs men swarmed over the large ships. They rowed slowly, toward a more ancient section of the harbour where small boats reeked of ancient fish while their occupants mended nets and addressed each other in equally pungent *koiné*.

Howie had acquired a minimum of Aramaic in the last week but this was his first contact with the language of the New Testament. How, he wondered, would they get by here?

Lillith, using the few Aramaic words Howie understood,

managed with much arm waving to explain that she would do the talking and that he had best pretend to be her slave.

Howie saw the wisdom of this: slaves were not expected to fight and these bruisers looked as if they'd like nothing better. They inched along the mole to a vacant space large enough for the caïque's bow. Howie scrambled over the slimy stones and tied up. By the time he had helped Lillith up onto the dock an immense crowd had gathered.

Howie glanced embarrassedly at his ragged dungarees. He must be wearing the only pants in town. He ran a hand over his sunburned chin and wondered when he'd find a razor to take off the half dozen bristles which sprouted there.

Lillith addressed the gawkers shrilly. Had Howie known more of the language he would have know her Greek was almost as atrocious as his Aramaic. But she got the idea across. Soon fishermen bid briskly against each other. One dumped a few *staters* and a large handful of copper *óboloi* into the pockets she made of her tattered skirt. She handed him the caïque's painter.

The crowd dispersed. Howie studied Lillith's legs and desire rose in him for the first time since they'd sailed. But there were too many people. Glancing about at the few women's long skirts, he saw Lillith was conspicuous, brazen, or both. He pointed at the money and at a pocket in his dungarees. Lillith gave him a swift glance and surrendered the coins.

She started down the narrow street and Howie, after she had hissed and pointed a couple of times, fell in behind as befitted a slave. The street was cobbled with uneven stones which threatened to sprain his ankle with every step. It was not over ten feet wide at best and upper floors extended until the street caught less than enough sunlight to dry the stinking mounds of rubbish and offal which collected beneath balconies.

The lower storey was mostly open-front, selling weird

things at whose use Howie could only guess. He muttered an unchristian word as his toe stubbed another cobble. Why hadn't he brought his shoes?

Lillith was used to going barefoot but she fared little better. Abruptly she stopped before a display of sandals. Moments later they had two pairs, and half of the copper coins were gone. A few doors farther they stopped again and Howie squatted for nearly an hour while Lillith tried on robes until she found one which showed off her sultry complexion to advantage.

In considerably less time she picked a *himation*. Howie put it on but refused to remove his trousers. Lillith, after some venomous asides, led the way again. Howie's denim-clad legs attracted stares from those Athenians who had not yet seen anything. He struggled with the *himation*. Lillith was suddenly walking much faster. Eventually, he got the bulky garment bunched up around his waist, more or less as others seemed to wear it.

They left the docks and the fishy smell was gradually displaced by an all-pervading odour of onion, garlic, and the rancid stink of olive oil. When had he eaten last, Howie wondered. The smell grew stronger and he felt suddenly faint. Lillith stopped so abruptly that he bumped into her and Howie saw that one of the open-fronted shops had an immense soot-blackened cauldron in which oil smoked and little brown things sizzled.

The cook was a small, suspicious man with kinky black hair. His eyes became human only when Lillith extracted money from the hypnotised Howie's pocket. Then the little man grabbed chunks of dough and twirled them pizza fashion before dumping fried sausage and a handful of onion in the midst of each. When each gob of dough was rolled back into a ball he dropped it in. Howie could not take his eyes from the cauldron. After an eternity of waiting for them to cool Howie and Lillith wandered on down the street, dodging porters, pack mules, and an occasional VIP's litter.

They were leaving Piraeus now, starting the six mile walk up between the remains of the famous long walls. Howie felt better since he had eaten. But with his stomach full, he became even more cognisant of how long it had been since he had last slept. Lillith had catnapped while he steered constantly. He looked wistfully for some place to sleep but every nook in the ruined walls was filled with lounging sailors, drovers, or bands of half-drunk students out picnicking.

Howie plodded behind, seething inwardly as students caught sight of Lillith and made loud remarks which required no translation.

Two miserable stumbling hours later they finished the uphill walk to Athens. Howie was so exhausted that he took no notice of the *stoa* through which they trudged, save that he was startled by the gaudily painted statue of a naked young man about to fling a plate at somebody. He had always thought statues were left in the natural white of marble.

Lillith stopped before a building which reeked of steam and oil. Well scrubbed men lounged before the building. Those downwind moved when Howie and Lillith sat down. The silver coins were all gone and only a handful of copper *óboloi* remained. Howie wondered if there'd be enough for a room in whatever these foreigners had in the way of a hotel. He was going over his meagre vocabulary, trying to find a way to ask Lillith, when he noticed a small, bright-eyed man studying them intently. Howie stared back. The little man's *chlamys* fit better than most of the citizenry's and was woven of finer material. Howie glanced at Lillith. She too had noticed the man's glance. Jealous anger boiled through Howie at the suspicion that they had been communicating for some time.

Abruptly, he remembered he was pretending to be a slave.

The sooner he got to Rome, the better, Howie decided. He didn't think he was going to like Greeks.

The little man moved toward them. Lillith gave Howie a warning glance and he lapsed into immobility. The conversation was long and repetitive, due to Lillith's imperfect Greek, but eventually the little man produced a silver *stater*. Other loungers gathered to watch the bargaining and offer ribald comment.

Lillith extracted the last of the money from Howie's pocket and spread it beside her. Pointing to coins and extending fingers, she indicated her price. Howie's anger disappeared, overwhelmed by a numbing shock. He was seeing Lillith in her true light for the first time—peddling herself like a common—He couldn't bring himself even to think the word.

The little man's eyes burned more brightly. He licked his full red lips. Lillith, with a gesture of finality, picked up her coins and tossed them down the front of her dress. The little man knew when he was licked. He produced a handful of *staters*. Howie's eyes bulged. He knew how much they'd gotten for the caïque and how far it had gone. But this—why, it must be ten times as much!

And she could make all this money just for . . . Lillith dumped the silver down the front of her dress. It was wrong, of course; she shouldn't do it. But then, they *did* need money. And it would only take a little while. He brightened as he reflected that he now had a steady source of income which could take them both to Rome. And since he was going to Rome for a good cause . . . Come to think of it, Jesus hadn't hesitated to accept Mary Magdalene's earnings.

Lillith pointed at the entrance of the building. He recognised the word for bath. Or was it wash? He'd have to make himself scarce anyway while Lillith performed her part of the bargain.

The bright-eyed little man propelled him toward the

bath attendant. Howie let himself be led into the first chamber. The attendant took his clothes and left him to doze in drowsy, comforting steam. He woke abruptly from a dream of carnal delights to discover the attendant scraping him with a *strigil*—like a wooden currycomb. After a while he was propelled into the next room, a swimming pool full of warm water. He joined the men who squatted there and fell asleep.

The attendant fished him out and slapped his back till he was through coughing and choking, then led him into the next room. The attendant pushed him into the cold pool. By the time he had splashed his way to the other end he was wide awake. To his surprise, the bright-eyed little man was waiting for him. Howie looked for his clothes but the little man had him by the hand and was leading him to a curtained-off alcove.

Thirty seconds later the little man burst through the curtains immediately in front of Howie's foot. 'Jehovah smite thee!' Howie raged. 'Isn't the girl enough? Jesus rescue me from this den of iniquity!'

The little man stood at a safe distance, lower lip trembling as he stared at this berserk apparition.

A crowd gathered immediately. Hadn't these Greeks anything to do but stare? One elderly man detached himself from the crowd and edged toward Howie. 'Didst say Jesus?' he asked.

Howie stared.

'Art thou Christian?' the old man continued. 'Methought thy tongue rang haply of mine own.'

'Who are you?' Howie croaked.

'Alas,' the old man sighed, 'once I was Brother Willibald of Glastonbury—until that Satan inspired Alchemist talked me into arming his copper coiled Alembic.' The old man sighed again. 'The Abbey may now possess the Philosophers' Stone and know all the Arts of transmuting Base Metals into Gold but alas—will Brother Willibald ever again drink the brown October Ale?'

'He paid her good money,' Howie said. 'What's he doing *here*?'

Brother Willibald smiled sadly. 'Alas, poor Wight,' he said. 'That Flower of Evil sold not herself. 'Tis thou who art sold!'

It was impossible; Lillith would not do such a thing! Then he remembered: it had been her idea that he pretend to be slave, her idea that he walk behind. Come to think of it, just about everything since she had broken him out of that cage aboard the *Alice* had been her idea. There was but one thing to do with people like Lillith. Through his chosen instrument, Howie, the Lord of Hosts would strike her dead.

He reached for the revolver and remembered he no longer had it. He had nothing—no sandals, no *chlamys*, not even his dungarees!

The old man still faced him, looking for all the world like Howie's Old Testament-tinted concept of the father he'd never had.

'Strooth, thou'rt sold,' Brother Willibald said. 'Wilt thou accept the Penance with true Christian Fortitude or wilt thou rail against the Path which thy God hath set thee?'

Brother Willibald's question took Howie unawares and abruptly shattered several of his more cherished illusions. Now, he finally remembered that his God had existed even before Christ. He was naked before his enemies, but not beyond jurisdiction. He was being punished by the merciful, compassionate, all powerful and eternal God—the Secret Named God of Abraham and Isaac, the God of Israel, God of Christ, God of Howie, God of Mercy, God of Vengeance.

He had been only too ready to sell, or at least rent, Lillith. Abruptly he burst into ragged cackling laughter. He was still giggling and whooping hysterically when the hot-eyed little man nudged him into the cold pool.

The chill sobered Howie. He climbed out considerably chastened to face his owner. 'I've sinned and I'll pay,' Howie said. 'I'll do whatever he says except one thing. Even God would never make me do that.'

Brother Willibald interpreted. The crowd marvelled at Howie's amusing display of foreign obstinacy with varying degrees of amusement and cynicism. The hot-eyed little man's lips began trembling again. He asked another question and when Brother Willibald answered at some length his shoulders drooped.

'He had no other Work for thee,' Brother Willibald interpreted.

Howie found it in his heart to be vaguely sorry for his owner. After all, Lillith had cheated both of them! Brightening, Howie turned to Brother Willibald. 'Maybe you could buy me?'

'God's Wounds!' the old man groaned. 'Had I such Gold I'd buy myself.'

Howie stared. 'Are you . . . ?' he began.

Brother Willibald sighed. 'I'd not been a day in this Cradle of Democracy before I was seized as a foreign Pauper and auctioned. Alack!' he sighed again, 'and never-more to taste the brown October Ale.' He mumbled incoherently for some moments, then noticed Howie again. 'Mayhap I'll resolve thy Plight,' he said. He spoke rapidly to Howie's owner. The hot-eyed little man nodded and shambled sadly back toward the hot room.

Brother Willibald found Howie's *chlamys* but misunderstood the young god shouter's demand for his pants. It did not occur to Howie to say trousers, hosen, or *bracae*. Resigned to the loss, he strapped on his sandals. Brother Willibald led him out of the baths and around the block, up a flight of stairs. There Brother Willibald knocked and the door was unbarred by the loveliest creature Howie had surveyed in all his eighteen years.

She was short, more petite than Lillith, and her diaphanous *stola* displayed a tiny waist beneath firm breasts. Her long black hair was in a single braid, piled voluptuously into a crown. The face beneath that crown looked on Howie with every indication of delight. She led Howie into the atrium and signalled him to wait.

'Who is she?' Howie asked.

'Doth Chloe please thee?'

Howie was too stricken to answer.

Brother Willibald smiled a small secret smile and said nothing.

Another woman entered the room. Though there wasn't the slightest resemblance, her stern, forbidding attitude reminded Howie of his mother. She surveyed the young god shouter from all angles, looked at his teeth, and questioned Brother Willibald.

By the time the old man turned and said, 'My Lady will buy thee,' Howie felt six inches shorter.

Remembering Chloe, Howie brightened. Brother Willibald showed him around and Howie tried to shake the girl from his mind long enough to remember which room was which. He was shown a pile of straw in the kitchen for the servants.

'How many are there?'

'Thou, I, the cook, and Chloe.'

Howie worried until the cook turned out to be a wall-eyed old crone with a slightly crooked back.

'Our Nightwatchman died,' Brother Willibald explained. ' 'Tis best that thou sleepest now.'

Considering the day's adventures, it was commendable for Howie's conscience that he lay awake all of thirty seconds. He had no way of knowing the hour when somebody shook him gently awake.

After mumbling incoherently and rubbing his eyes he saw

Chloe, more desirable than ever, carrying a lamp which looked like a shallow teapot with a wick coming out the spout. It silhouetted her lithe young body beneath the transparent *stola*.

She led him from the kitchen's discordant snores. They tiptoed across the atrium to another room and Chloe blew out the lamp. Howie groped blindly before his questioning hands found her again. She had removed her *stola* and rubbed against him in pristine nakedness.

Howie shucked his *chlamys* and they performed mutual explorations. Preliminaries ended abruptly and matters became more serious.

Two hours' sleep were not enough to make up for forty-eight hours without. Some minutes later those exploring hands shook Howie rather abruptly. He yawned and sighed in the darkness, remembering the daylight glimpse of Chloe. Again the night-game began. The farther it progressed the more puzzled Howie became. Chloe was small, with smooth firm flesh. Could these tremendous buttocks be hers? Would her belly wrinkle and droop? Could those firm breasts yield like masses of unbaked bread beneath his fingers?

He retreated to his side of the bed and sat, trying not to vomit. Was it the walleyed cook? No; she was shorter than Chloe. With a sinking feeling, Howie realised he had traded a master for a mistress.

He was feeling sorry for himself when he remembered Brother Willibald's remark about penance.

'I got myself into this,' Howie gritted. 'I'll get myself out!' He threw himself back into bed and cleaved unto the unknown quantity.

Then something like a wet sandbag hit him in the small of the back and he knew no more.

On the *Alice*, all hands were gazing anxiously at the two Liburnians. 'Go below!' Joe shouted. 'We're going to jump and I don't want anybody washed overboard.'

'Who steers?' Gorson asked.

'I do. Freedy, you ready?' he yelled down the scuttle.

'All ready, sir.'

The sail was all in, piled on deck in untidy mounds. Time enough to furl it if the jump was successful. The Liburnians quickstroked and Joe knew they could, for a short time anyhow, make better time than the *Alice* under power. The jump had damned well better work! 'All right,' he yelled, 'throw the switch!'

The twisting, wrenching sensation was over in one subliminal flicker, like a misplaced frame in a movie. The Liburnians had disappeared; the *Alice* was now in broad daylight and a calm sea.

Then he noticed Howard McGrath. The little god shouter was tangled in a heap of sail, and as he regained consciousness he began again his befogged and half-hearted attempts at lovemaking. Only when his head had cleared completely did he realise that the unaesthetic heap of sail was not his recently-acquired mistress. Howie stopped suddenly, and stared around at the speculative, amused faces of his shipmates as they straggled up on deck.

Howie's return was the last thing Joe had expected at that moment. Afterward he tried to analyse what went on inside his head at that moment. The young god shouter's appearance neither surprised nor mystified him. It must have been the sudden fruitation of long unconscious cerebration—a mushroom of knowledge which burst into awareness after days of patient, probing subterranean growth. In other words, intuition.

Sympathetic magic, Joe sneered, for his explanation was about as scientific as sticking pins in dolls or removing warts with separated bean halves. But, magic or not, Joe knew Howie had returned because he was part of the original ship's company. Something—aura, field, mystique held them together and strove to replace everything sooner or later back into its own proper time.

Joe thought of the teeming mass of time mongrels below-decks with a little shiver of foreboding.

'Where are we?' Gorson asked.

'Search me,' Joe said. 'At least we're away from those f . . .' He stopped horrorstricken at the realisation that he had been about to modify 'Liburnians' with a present part-iciple unbecoming an officer, gentleman, or professor of history. He'd have to watch himself if he ever hoped to lecture again.

Raquel came on deck '¿Cuándo esamos?' she asked Joe. was amused that her precise Latin mind asked not where, but *when* they were. She stood upwind and her usual gamy stink was replaced by a fresh, unperfumed odour of healthy female. Joe remembered the oarmaster's explana-tion of her former fetors and grinned.

Freedy's tiny mouth formed a report. 'Everything looks fine. Still's in one piece. Nothing on the radio though; I swept every band.'

Joe sighed, then brightened. After all, it had taken two jumps to get here. Maybe something limited them to thousand-year jumps. If so, they must be roughly back in Raquel's time. He looked around again. The sea rippled under a full sail breeze which drove them gently toward a bright, half-high sun. A slight ground swell hinted at shallow water but there was neither land nor breakers. He looked at the compass and tried to fix the time of day.

It didn't look right. Reaching into the binnacle, he wiggled the gimbals. It wasn't stuck. He spun the wheel and the compass card swung obligingly. He eased back on course and looked at the sun again. The weather was too balmy; he wasn't in the Arctic. Where else could the sun swing so far north?

He groaned.

'What's wrong?' Cookie asked.

Joe pointed at the compass. 'Ah don't git it.'

Gorson crowded up and peered into the binnacle. 'I do,' he said sickly.

'Right,' Joe said, 'Only Mahan knows where, but we're in the southern hemisphere.'

Gorson sighed tiredly. 'You guys furl those sails,' he said.

Joe nodded. 'Run the jib and jigger up for steerageway.' He turned the wheel over to Guilbeau and went below.

Raquel stood in the doorway in his cubicle, silently watching as he pored over inadequate charts, looking for any salt water in the southern hemisphere which lay out of sight of land and shallow enough for a ground swell. The southern hemisphere was mostly water and they could be just about anywhere.

'You worry?' Raquel asked.

Joe turned to explain. 'Do you know the world is round?' he asked.

'I have heard it said.'

'Do you believe it?'

She shrugged. 'I am still not sure whether I believe in you.'

'Well, anyhow,' Joe said, 'I'm not sure when we are. Maybe in your own time. But we're on the wrong side of the world.'

'What will you do?'

He shrugged. 'Keep trying. What else can I do? I'm sorry I couldn't take you home.'

'Home?'

'Your own time. Wouldn't you like to see your parents again? Didn't you have a young man before you left home?'

It was Raquel's turn to sigh. 'So long . . .' she said. 'I had no thought of ever seeing home again. Perhaps they still live.'

'The young man?'

'Man? Ah; I had no *novio*. Once a boy stood below my window. My father investigated. His family was not suitable so the boy was told not to walk down our street again.'

Cook produced rye bread and dried goat stew. All hands crowded in the galley. 'So now what?' Dr. Krom asked.

Joe explained his theorising about thousand-year jumps.

'What proof have you?' the old man asked.

'As much that I'm right as you have that I'm wrong,' Joe said, and silently damned the quibbling old man. Holy Neptune but he was tired! Would he ever get enough sleep?

Abe Rose choked down a lump of stringy meat and cleared his throat. Behind the black whiskers his mouth was slightly lopsided as though still cramped around an imaginary cigar. 'Why not jump again and see if we can pick up something on the radio?' he asked.

Joe was tempted to turn in but remembered what a night's sleep had cost him the last time. 'Square away the galley and set up the still,' he said.

He went on deck again. The ground swell was unchanged and there was still no land. The sun was slightly lower and farther left so he guessed it was mid-afternoon. Time jumps were getting his stomach as confused as jet travel. Raquel appeared and they faced each other across the lashed wheel. 'You are tired,' she said.

Joe agreed. 'That's the principal recompense for being captain.'

'You did not wish to take the other girls,' she pursued.

'No,' Joe agreed.

'Why did you take me?'

'Why uh . . . Well, you saved my life.'

'Is that all?'

'What can you expect?' Joe asked. 'Admittedly, love at first sight is a great time saver, but I'd known you all of five minutes when you came aboard.' He paused. This wasn't coming out the way he meant it to. How could he explain his gradual growth of confidence—his increasing ease in her simple, often pointless conversation? 'After a time . . .' he began. What he wanted to say was how nice it was to be around someone who was quiet when he needed silence—someone who made no demands nor expected him to solve all problems. He glanced up and she was gone. 'Damn it!' If she had just stuck around another moment he felt sure he would have found a way to say it. Oh well, some day he'd have more time.

The horizon was clear, the sea calm. At last they would be making a jump under less than frantic circumstances. This time Joe would be below, watching every dial and meter. Sooner or later he would control this phenomenon.

Dishes were cleared away. Inside its makeshift bell jar the still sat amidships of the galley table. The *Alice*'s crew and Ma Trimble crowded into an attentive circle. The blondes regarded the prospect of another jump with monumental apathy. They scattered about the yawl, fixing each other's hair, mending clothing. Up by the chain locker one blonde unravelled a tattered jersey. Joe wondered what she intended with the yarn. Not socks for sure; the Mediterraneans hadn't invented them yet.

'All set,' Gorson reported. He jumped over the vacuum pump. Cookie regarded the bell jar and slapped a dough patch over one point where the seal threatened to rupture.

Joe felt his stomach tighten. Would they materialise in the middle of a desert? Or a hundred feet above or below it? 'You may fire when ready,' he said.

Freedy flipped the switch. Nothing happened. They waited for tubes to warm up. Still nothing. Freedy flipped the gang switch up to middle range and began cranking up the pot. Abruptly, vision shimmered for a microsecond and Joe felt that now-familiar twisting, as if gravity had gone off for half a heartbeat.

The blondes glanced up from their hair fixing. The girl

174

unravelling a sweater up by the chain locker had disappeared. Up on deck, Joe guessed. He went up through the after scuttle and for a moment wondered if he hadn't imagined the twisting sensation. The *Alice* still sailed herself under jib and jigger, beating gently toward the sun in a calm sea. Then he noticed: the groundswell was gone—they were in deep water!

Judging from the cloudless sky, they must be well offshore. He glanced at the binnacle and released a long-held breath. They were in the northern hemisphere.

It was the emptiest ocean Joe had ever seen. The sky had a strange, leaden colour and the sun shone like molten brass. Gently rippling water stretched in all directions toward a horizon which curved upward until the *Alice* seemed alone at the bottom of an immensely empty blue bowl. Which ocean? Joe wondered. There was not a bird in the sky, nor a weed in the water. He took a final glance round and went below.

Gorson and Cookie had dismantled the bell jar so it was safe to turn on the other gear. 'Three hundred and ten fathoms,' Freedy reported. 'No scattering layer.'

'Tried the radio?' Joe asked.

Freedy's little mouth flew open. 'Hadn't thought of it,' he confessed, and flipped switches. Joe waited not very hopefully for the set to warm up. He knew there were immense stretches of practically sterile ocean, yet something about that absolute emptiness worried him. Maybe he'd read too many stories of atomic doom, but if he had overshot and landed ahead of his own time . . . He wished there were a geiger counter aboard the *Alice*.

Gorson nudged him and pointed at the barometer. Abruptly, Joe understood the emptiness and that weird yellow light, the absence of birds. How many hours did he have? He tried to remember what he knew about hurricanes and typhoons. According to the barometer this was going to be the granddaddy of them all.

The radio warmed up and Freedy started at the shortest band. Aside from clicks and pops of atmospheric electricity, nothing came in. Then Howard McGrath was pulling Joe's sleeve.

Still wearing nothing but a pair of borrowed skivvy drawers, he hunched his shoulders and humped his thin body unhappily. 'Mr. Rate,' he whispered, and glanced about embarrassedly. 'Mr. Rate,' he whispered again, more urgently now, 'it hurts when I pee.'

Joe clapped a hand to his forehead. Closing eyes tighty, he searched for an adequate phrase. None came. He lowered his hand and his elbow caught Ma Trimble in the ribs. 'Talk yourself out of this one,' he growled.

'My girls were clean when they came aboard,' Ma Trimble snapped. 'You think I don't know the signs?'

Joe turned to Howie. The god shouter swallowed and looked miserable. 'I don't know, sir,' he said. 'Maybe it was Chloe, or the old lady. You see, I . . .'

'Spare me the details,' Joe groaned. 'You must've really spread that old gospel around.' He turned to Ma Trimble, who still huffed like a catscratched bulldog. 'You've had the experience,' he said. 'You can hold shortarm inspection.'

Freedy still gaped at the unhappy god shouter. 'Well?' Joe asked.

The minuscule mouthed radioman went back to twirling knobs. Abruptly he pursed his lips and stopped. After a moment the fuzzy, faintly audible noise broke into dots and dashes. Joe could not recognise a single letter. Freedy was also puzzled. Gorson abruptly took charge. 'Get a fix!' he snapped, and reached for the direction finder.

Joe rushed into his cubicle, then returned. He couldn't lay out a line of position unless he knew where the signal came from. 'Can you read it?' he asked.

Gorson gave him a wry look. 'No, but I know what it is.'

Joe waited.

'Kana code,' the bos'n grunted. 'Imperial Japanese Navy Headquarters, Tokyo.'

'What year we in?' Cookie asked. 'You s'pose we're still at war?'

'Unless it hasn't started yet,' Gorson said. 'I led the working party that blew up that transmitter.'

Freedy switched to another band. Minutes later the RDF left them in no doubt of their position. The *Alice* lay between thirty-six and thirty-eight degrees north, and approximately a hundred and sixty degrees west. The transmitters were too far away to get a closer bearing but no one cared. A thousand miles north of the Hawaiian Islands there was little chance of running aground or into anything else, save possibly the Japanese fleet. It was New Year's Day, 1942.

12

They faced each other, stunned. They had followed the yawl's meanderings uncomplainingly throughout anquity but a mere twenty years staggered them. Somewhere at this minute, Joe thought, my mother's wheeling me around in a stroller. My father is just about to be swindled out of his partnership in the restaurant.

Gorson broke off the reverie of his own hectic life in the early days of the war. 'What do we do now?' he asked.

Joe glanced around at Ma Trimble's blondes and felt an unreasoning anger at the casualness with which they combed, mended, and chattered. Might as well get one thing over, he thought. 'All hands assemble for a short-arm inspection. Ma Trimble's the expert.' He retreated to his cubicle and closed the door.

1942. He couldn't stay here, he knew. Joe had read extensively in the newspaper files of this period. If the *Alice* showed up in any American port they'd all rot in prison camp while some birdbrained bureaucrat tried to figure the angles behind the Axis sending out a load of saboteurs with such a weird cover story.

No, not even in prison, Joe decided. They'd be lucky if they weren't shot.

And that miserable god shouting eightball had managed to get himself a dose. Even if there had been any medicaments aboard the yawl Joe would have been afraid to use them. He reviewed all his theories, hunches, and superstitions about time travel.

They were about twenty years from their starting point —which, all things considered, was pretty good. So far he had learned how to separate forward from reverse. He wondered if further refinements were possible and wished he could understand what Einstein had said about time. Damn it, if only he could learn to separate logic from magic in his thinking!

What was time? All this talk of rhythms and streams and fourth dimensions sounded to Joe like the learned balderdash of scientasters who concealed their ignorance behind Greek-rooted redundancies. Whatever it was, only one time really existed for Joe, for the *Alice* and for the *Alice's* original company. That was their own time: mid-twentieth century. Everything else was history and no matter how real to those who lived in it, it would never be real to Joe. Only 1965 was his.

The future was equally nonexistent, except as a series of extrapolations—a branching of possibilities, a budding of possibilities from the only true and real time: Joe's present.

If the future were equally nonexistent to the machine, perhaps it would not or could not venture forward beyond its own time.

But it was confusing. Did Raquel and these blondes and all the others know they had been living in the past? Probably not. It was their present and only the past for Joe. Maybe a machine built in their time would reject any later era as impossible or unreal. If so they could jump again and cut down the remaining distance to their own era!

Joe smiled momentarily. They could still make that Saturday inspection. But, he sobered, there was not one shred of evidence to prove his theory. Well, what could he lose? Not much, considering that typhoon was due any time now.

Holy Neptune! He'd forgotten about the barometer and that brassy sky. He opened the cubicle door and brushed past Ma Trimble as she tried to say something.

It was dead calm now, without a sniff of wind. The late afternoon sun was an immense flaming ball, as if no protective atmosphere separated if from the *Alice*. The sea had a sluggish, oily look and the *Alice*'s sails slatted gently as she rocked in an old swell which came from the south-east. In the direction of the swell the horizon was different—as if some gigantic hand had pried sky and sea apart and was now driving a thin black wedge in between.

Joe glanced absently at his wrist. Damn those watch-stealing Romans! How much time had he? He went below and after one unbelieving glance at the barometer yelled for Gorson and Cookie. 'Set up the still—make it quick!'

Gorson and Cookie stared dumbly, with eyes like cata-tonic spaniels. The rest of the crew was mute and worried Ma Trimble was solemn. 'Well, what's wrong?' Joe snapped. '*Everybody* got a dose?'

Ma Trimble shook her head and her chins quivered. She dabbed at her eyes with an oversized man's handkerchief. Gorson cleared his throat and swallowed a couple of times. 'Three girls gone,' he said. 'No sign of them anywhere. Abishag, Miriam . . .'

'Abishag—she was the one who was unravelling a jersey?'

Rose nodded unhappily and held out a ball of yarn.

Joe remembered how the girl had disappeared at the moment of the jump. He thought she'd gone on deck. Why hadn't all the girls gravitated back to their own time, just as Howie had been snatched back to his?

The bell jar and coil must set up a field. Close to it, you're safe, but get so far away . . . The girl had been lean-ing against the chain locker bulkhead—almost in the *Alice*'s bows. Abruptly, Joe stopped, realising what news they were trying to break to him. He drew a deep breath and looked for a place to sit.

'Gorson nodded. 'Yeah,' he said. 'Raquel too.'

'You're sure?' he finally asked, and knew they were. Damn it, why did she have to go now? Up on deck awhile ago he'd been—well, what? It wasn't . . . He sighed. Well, it just wasn't fair. He could see it all now. She hung out in the chain locker. Whenever things went wrong she crawled into her hole just as he crawled into his cubicle. Why hadn't he guessed earlier why she flaunted that gamy stink? More important, he should have realised what those intervals of cleanliness meant. If he had said the right things she wouldn't have run off to the chain locker. Why had he put it off?

He felt his insides tense at the anticipation of pain. It was going to hurt, he knew. Each day the aching would grow and swell. The emptiness inside him would grow until one day the thin shell would crumple and there would be nothing left of Joe. He wondered what the crew of the *Alice* would do if he were to tear his hair and scream quadrilingual blasphemies.

'Sir,' Gorson was saying, 'the barometer . . .'

Holy hell, the typhoon!

Someday he would have time to mourn. Someday her name would be graven with letters of fire in some dark and secret corner of his duodenum. But for the time being he was captain of the *Alice*.

'Guilbeau, Rose, Schwartz, and Villegas, on deck! Take in all sail. Dog everything down ready to jump. Gorson and Cook, rig the still. Freedy, you know what to do.'

He went on deck. The giant was prying horizon and sea farther apart. The black wedge could not be more than minutes away from the *Alice*. 'Step lively with that sail!' he yelled, and began lashing the wheel.

Instructions were unnecessary. The *Alice*'s people knew the weather and their captain were both ready to break. 'I 'won't think about it,' Joe muttered, and helped punch the tattered mains'l into a neat furl. *There isn't time to think.* He took a final look at that widening black wedge before following his people down the after scuttle.

The deck was secured, the hatches dogged. Gorson and Cookie were at the still. Freedy's hands poised over the fathometer. 'Everything set where it was last jump?' Joe asked. Freedy nodded. 'All right, let's try it.'

The switch clicked and all hands waited for the warmup. Joe reviewed all the countless possibilities for disaster. *I won't think about her.* So far the *Alice* had always fetched up afloat. Did their time machine have a special fondness for salt water or was each jump straining the law of averages? Five continents and seven seas; you pays yer money and you takes yer choice. *I won't think about her.*

Nothing was happening.

'Move back to zero,' Joe said, 'and start ranging out again.'

'Right,' Freedy grunted. The instant his hand touched the knob Joe felt that now familiar twisting. Past, present, future? At least they were at sea. The *Alice* was rocking violently. He'd better get on deck and set a little canvas to steady her.

Two jumps away from her now. Did she land safely or spend her final hour treading water lonely leagues from land? I won't think . . . His head emerged from the scuttle and he found himself staring at a blank grey wall. He glanced up straight into horrified faces which stared down at him from the deck of a destroyer. The destroyer was at flank speed, passing the *Alice's* port side with barely four feet to spare. He glanced about and realised even this horror could be magnified.

Six destroyers had been steaming two abreast. Now they were peeling off at impossible angles as radar or bow lookouts sighted the *Alice*. The last destroyer in the starboard column had apparently not gotten the word; her knifelike bow pointed unerringly at the *Alice*'s mizzen mast. She was a length and a half away, making all of twenty-two knots!

Joe dived down the after scuttle, scattering the blondes who headed up it. Thank Neptune the bell jar was still set up. The red pilot light glowed on the fathometer. Brushing Freedy aside, he spun the range selector. All hands poured on deck to see what had spooked him.

Cringing against the crash to come, Joe spun the dial frantically. Agonising seconds passed before he again felt the shimmering flicker which meant they had jumped. Was he getting used to time travel or was the sensation getting weaker? *Three jumps away from her.*

He stuck his head out of the scuttle, wondering what new disaster would present itself. The *Alice*'s crew stood and sat in various attitudes of numbed stupefaction. Gorson struggled to his feet when he saw Joe. 'That tin can,' he croaked. 'I know those guys!' The chief's eyes were show-too much white. 'Jesus!' he muttered, and began wilting. Joe caught him and lowered the bos'n gently. *So he knows them.* Had he known them a month ago or twenty years ago? The tin cans looked fairly recent but . . . Abruptly Joe remembered the telltale bulge of a piece of super-secret electronic gear. That gadget hadn't been operational six months ago.

The sun had an early morning look and, after a glance at the compass, he decided they were still in the northern hemisphere. Freedy still mumbled and counted his fingers. Joe gave him a despairing glance and went below. After turning on the fathometer and letting air into the bell jar he turned on the radio. *Is she alive somewhere?*

This time the air was full—not just short and long wave, but all the UHF and VHF channels which had not existed twenty years ago. Down in one corner someone was single sidebanding. These return jumps were apparently a logarithmic progression. Or was that it? Each one, at any rate, grew shorter as they approached their own time. He wondered if he were days or weeks away. Chances were that lessened twisting sensation meant this last jump away from the destroyer had only covered a week or two.

He found a news broadcast and began swinging the direction finder. Mellifluous, pear-shaped tones revealed territorial encroachments on five continents. Fine Italian hands penned notes in Cyrillic to the Secretary-General

Joe decided he was either due east or west of the transmitter. When would that mealy-mouthed commentator shut up long enough for station identification? He glanced absently at his wrist. Damn those Romans!

Abe Rose came down the after scuttle. 'I see we're home,' he grunted.

'How do you know?'

Rose gave a humourless *hah*. 'I'd know that prevaricating son of an unnatural union between Barry Goldwater and Daddy Warbucks if I heard him in Katmandu. And considering the wattage on which he defiles us Democrats, I'd say we aren't a hundred miles from San Diego.'

Howard McGrath came below, looking pale and unhappy. He was followed by Dr. Krom, who helped Ma Trimble down the scuttle. Tears shimmered in her eyes. 'All gone but Ruthie,' she sniffled. 'We'll be next.'

Ruthie—that was the blonde who'd shared Villegas' bunk. Again Joe was reminded of Raquel.

'. . . and so we come to the end of KLOD's political powwow for this day, March 2, 1965 . . .'

March 2 . . . why, tomorrow was the day . . . Commander Cutlott's crowd would be holding inspection. And oh God, what a mess the *Alice* was in! Foul-bottomed, topside paint peeling, spear, axe and catapult scars in her deck, half her gear missing and the other half rotten. . . .

'All hands turn to,' he yelled. 'We've got to get this bucket shipshape.'

He'd have to go over the yawl from stem to stern and get rid of anything the blondes had left. Things were going to be hard enough to explain without getting into that right off! He'd start with the lazerette, which was just about as far as he could get from the chain locker. *I won't think of her.*

The lazerette was empty. Joe stared. The last time he'd looked it'd been full of sacked rye. Then he realised what happened. With each jump the *Alice*'s hold on these extratemporal articles had become more tenuous. Finally, they had gone the way of the girls, the way of . . . He climbed down into the compartment to see if a dress or sandal had been left behind.

The lazerette was empty, save for Gorson's and Cookie's immense foot lockers. Why they needed these empty trunk-sized boxes aboard ship he would never know unless . . . No, he'd looked several times and they'd always been empty.

Well, they were nearly back to normal. All the *Alice*'s original people were aboard. There remained only Ma Trimble and one blonde to explain away. Villegas could sneak them ashore before inspection time.

Howard McGrath was looking down into the lazerette. 'Mr. Rate,' he complained. 'I can't hardly pee at all!'

'I'm fresh out of aspirin. Have you tried prayer?' Joe climbed out of the lazerette and hesitated as he saw how utterly crushed the young god shouter was. 'Oh, keep your shirt on,' he growled. 'You'll be in a naval hospital in twelve hours. When you get out I'll see if I can't get you a medal.' He glared into the mist. When could Point Loma loom up through the coastal fog?

Why'm I poking around like this? he wondered. Gorson had enough sense to get anything incriminating out of sight before inspection. He went into his cubicle and opened the 'want book' and inventory sheets. How would he ever make them come out? *I won't think of her.*

He buried his head in his hands. He should, he supposed, be thankful it had ended this way. After all, how could she have fitted into faculty life in a college town? Like it or not, he was a professor. Subconsciously, he had always known he would never make a career of the navy. He had had his little fling; now he would tuck his tail between his legs and scuttle back quietly into Dr. Battlement's History Department. He'd be a year behind his contemporary bright young men so far as seniority and tenure went, but . . . *I won't think of her.*

The *Alice's* motion had changed. He stripped the makeshift curtains (something else to replace before inspection) from his tiny porthole and saw a tug drift slowly past the *Alice*. There was a gentle bump as someone fended off. He was ready to go on deck when some instinct made him hesitate. What was Gorson up to? Why hadn't the bos'n warned him they were sighting someone?

Straining his head against the bulkhead, he caught a wall-eyed glimpse of a scow piled high with unsmeltable bits of antique aircraft, electronics gear too obsolete to be useful but too secret to be surplused to the unsuspecting public who paid for it. The after part of the scow was nearly awash with cases of shells and small arms ammo. While Joe watched, a small crane lifted two foot lockers from the *Alice* and strained two identical but much heavier boxes back aboard the yawl.

'Oh fine!' Joe muttered. He'd finally found out what Commander Cutlott wanted to know. His future was assured if he wanted it. What was in the two foot lockers? Something the navy was quite willing to heave overboard but which could land the bos'n and Cook in Mare Island for turning a fast buck at less cost to Uncle than some retired admiral's perfectly legal lobbying.

How did they intend to get the loot ashore? Didn't they realise the kind of going-over this poor old bucket would get tomorrow? Commander Cutlott had been awfully nice about finding a boot ensign a job, but Joe didn't see how he could throw Gorson and Cookie to the wolves after all they'd been through together. He'd have to warn them to jettison the stuff before they reached San Diego.

It was nearly dawn before the coast came into sight. In spite of the foghorn's twin-toned blat and the lighthouse's glimmer they crisscrossed the entrance several times before picking up the last buoy. The *Alice* began her slow way up the channel.

When they finally docked at 0900 a schooner twice as large as the *Alice* was crowded into the slip opposite. Joe gave her a look of fleeting envy. The *Baleen* had been built specifically for oceanographic work, with a fibreglass hull impervious to rocks, rot or worms. She was furnished with everything to keep forty men in fresh-water showered comfort for six months at a stretch. Why couldn't he have had something like that? Joe wondered. He sighed, consoling himself that she was twice as cumbersome and no faster than the weddy-bottomed *Alice*.

He trotted down the dock to the guard shack and telephoned for a corpsman to haul the god shouter and his gonococci off to the Naval Hospital. Then he stopped at Ship's Service long enough to buy soap and razor blades for all hands. By the time he got back, he hoped Villegas would have the two women out of the way.

There was still a faint wine-pink tint to the water in spite of the hose from the dockside which was now topping up their tanks. A faint hum of blower told him the galley stove was again operating on oil. He guessed Rose had promoted enough hose to make that connection too.

There was still an hour before Commander Cutlott's inspection party was due. They'd all be at least shaved by then. Coming out of the shower, he twitched his nose unbelievingly. Could that be real coffee? He went to the urn and drew a cup. Wonders of wonders, it was! 'Where'd you get stores already?' he asked.

Cookie glanced furtively at the mountain of supplies waiting to be stowed aboard the larger ship. Joe grinned.

187

The *Baleen* would never miss a couple of pounds. He hurried into his cubicle and struggled into a dress uniform. It hung sacklike and he realised how much weight he'd lost —how much they'd all lost, come to think of it.

He went on deck and saw Commander Cutlott at the end of the dock. The commander, his adjutant and yeoman were accompanied by a captain and a rear admiral.

Villegas hissed from the lazarette hatch. 'Cover it up, sir,' he said.

'You'll suffocate,' Joe whispered.

'Please sir, cover *us* up!'

'Oh no!' Joe groaned.

Commander Cutlott walked briskly down the dock, wearing a smile which became fixed as he came closer to the battered, unpainted yawl. By the time he boarded the *Alice* he was not smiling. After a round of saluting he got down to business. 'Well, Mr. Rate,' he snapped, 'did you find what we were looking for?'

Joe hadn't expected Commander Cutlott to sound off in front of everyone about the looting problem. He was still fumbling for an answer when he noticed the strange captain's face go through an astonishing transformation. Odd, Joe thought, I've never really seen a face turn purple before.

'You!' the captain roared. 'Gallivanting around in a restricted area, interfering with manœuvres . . .'

Joe remembered Commander Cutlott's warning: Gorson and Cookie had been using the ship for drunken ladyfests. He remembered how naked blondes had poured out on deck to watch the destroyers sheer off and several things were suddenly clear.

The admiral was giving him a long, hard look. 'Tell me, young man,' he asked, 'how do you put up that many women on a ship of this size?'

'What I'd like to know,' the captain added, 'is how you pulled that razzle dazzle on our radar? There wasn't a blip two seconds before I spotted you. I spent four hours looking for survivors!'

Commander Cutlott glared unbelievingly at his protégé. 'I speak more in sorrow than in anger,' he said. 'Where are they?'

'Who, sir?' Joe asked.

'The women, damn it! Up with that hatch!'

'Hatch, sir?'

'The one you're standing on.'

'Would you like to inspect the galley, sir?'

'No, I would not like to inspect the galley, sir. Now, up with the hatch!'

Resignedly, Joe stood aside. Freedy and Commander Cutlott's yeoman stooped to lift the hatch.

Seaman Villegas, Ma Trimbles and Ruth sat on two immense foot lockers and blinked into the sudden sun. Villegas still wore the tattered dungaress which had lasted him throughout the *Alice's* peregrinations. Though his smooth face scarcely required shaving, his overlength hair sufficed to give the Mexican a faintly piratical aspect.

Ruth wore the illfitting remnant of one of Raquel's dresses. She had ripped the skirt off at mid thigh. Whenever she sat it hiked considerably higher. But the inspecting party's attention focused on Ma Trimble's quivering bulk. 'Hello, boys,' she said brightly.

The admiral looked at Joe.

'Shipwrecked,' Joe began. 'We had to . . .'

'Oh, stow it!' the admiral growled. 'Which one of you has the Oedipus complex?'

A navy vehicle parked at the dock end and a sailor in whites walked towards the *Alice*. 'This where I'm supposed to pick up somebody with a dose of clap?' he yelled.

13

The sun sank in the west. Gorson stretched and decided they'd done enough painting for one day. He went below to see how Joe was making out with the ship's accounts. 'It could be worse, sir,' he said comfortingly.

'How?' Joe wondered. The god shouter's infirmity had gotten him off to the naval hospital. Jack Lapham and Dr. Krom had stood on their constitutional rights as civilians and stalked angrily ashore. Ma Trimble and her sole remaining blonde were off somewhere being questioned. Joe could guess what would happen. They'd deport the blonde to Tijuana and the Mexicans would depart her right back when it turned out she couldn't speak Spanish either. And wouldn't they have a great time making sense out of whatever story Ma Trimble told them!

The rest of the *Alice*'s crew was restricted, pending investigation. There might be no liberty for a long time, providing no one believed Ma Trimble's story. And if someone did, *l'affaire Alice* would be stamped *TOP SECRET* and their restriction might be even longer. *I won't think*—but he couldn't stop thinking of Raquel. Why did romantic novels always harp about heart and soul? It was the abdomen which felt the pangs of unrequited love. Already the empty feeling was changing into that nervous churning which would soon mean ulcer. 'How could things be worse?' he repeated.

The bos'n grinned around his first cigar in two thousand

years. 'Well,' he said, 'at least they didn't open the foot lockers.'

Joe slapped a hand to his forehead. 'Over the side, quick!'

'Come see what's in them.'

Joe followed the bos'n aft to the lazarette and watched while he opened one. Neatly wrapped in waterproof paper lay a disassembled machine gun. The space around it was taken up with two tommy guns, a dozen carbines, and Neptune knew how many pistols. Joe gasped. 'You guys planning a revolution?' he asked.

Gorson shook his head. 'No, but we know an Indonesian capitalist who is.'

'What's in the other box?'

'Ammo.'

Joe released an explosive breath. 'You've convinced me,' he said. 'It could have been worse!' His eye strayed about the dimly lit dock as Gorson slammed the foot locker and locked it. He eyed the mountain of groceries still waiting to be loaded aboard the *Baleen*. Careless of them. Nor was there any use telling his own people to leave them alone; they'd lived too long on rye bread. Besides, the *Alice*'s inventory had to be balanced somehow.

A suit of sails in clean new bags lay jumbled with the mountain of groceries. Gods, how he could have used some canvas for the Alice! He wondered how much trimming it would take to make them fit. Oh well—if only we could plan things and make them work out according to plan . . . He wondered if Raquel were alive somewhere. Maybe she'd landed back in her own time or even, remembering how Howie had landed back aboard the *Alice*, could she have gravitated back aboard the Iceland-bound *knarr* whence he had rescued her?

The moon broke through clouds and balanced itself atop the Cortez Hotel's lighted elevator shaft. It reminded him of their last night on the nameless volcanic island. Could he recognise its altered outline after two thousand years? Big deal! As if the navy'd ever send him to the Aegean again.

As a history professor . . . He saw himself taking a sabbatical thirty years from now, doddering about Greece on a budget tour, wondering if the cheese would agree with his ulcer. Another pang shot through his insides.

He sat a silent moment, remembering Raquel and those wasted moments in the chain locker. Anger boiled over and threatened to leak around his eyes. If only he could do it over again—only do it right this time!

Abruptly, a new thought seeped into his hindsighted reverie. He looked up and saw the chief still standing. Gorson studied him with a most peculiar expression on his broad face.

'Chief,' Joe said, 'do you still have that bell jar and still hidden somewhere?'

Gorson looked around the newly painted *Alice*. His eyes took in the *Baleen's* mountain of yearlong supplies, then rested for a moment on the foot lockers loaded with guns and ammunition. He grinned. 'I was wondering how long it'd take you to think of that,' he said.